SHAMELESS
HONEYMOON

SHAMELESS HONEYMOON

THOMAS STONE

CUTTING EDGE

Previously published as "A Talent for Love"

ISBN-13: 978-1-962896-93-1

Published by
Cutting Edge Books
PO Box 8212
Calabasas, CA 91372
www.cuttingedgebooks.com

CHAPTER ONE

M ADAME WAS in such a rage, it wouldn't have surprised Kathy in the least had she started foaming at the mouth.

"You little Greenwich Village tramp, you. *Get out.*"

She stood at the door of the little dressing room where Kathy was changing to her street clothes. The room was separated from the salon by a long, narrow hall, so it was unlikely that any of Yvette's wealthy customers would hear her angry shrieks. "You insult and kick my best customer. You are a fool. You're fired."

"I heard you the first time," Kathy replied cooly. "I wouldn't wonder if half of Fifth Avenue heard you. Must you yell so, just because one of our wolfish bankers liked my curves, and his old crow of a wife didn't care for the way he liked them? So I'm fired."

Kathy slipped her frock over her dark head and laughed. "It was quite an experience. I wouldn't have missed it for worlds. I'll never forget Mrs. Whittaker's look of astonishment when I kicked her in the shins. And the way she cried, *Ouch.* I think her husband got quite a kick out of it." Kathy laughed again. "The way I've got him figured, he's been itching to give her a couple of swift kicks on his own, but never got up the nerve to do it."

The girl's airy amusement in the face of adversity seemed to infuriate Yvette more than before, if that were possible. Vulgarly, for one who was supposed to be among the great as the extremely expensive French modiste deemed herself to be, Yvette set her hands to her hips, her arms akimbo.

"Shut up," she snapped. "How dare you talk like that about Mrs. Charley Whittaker, my richest customer! And you drive her out of my shop, because you seem to imagine modeling is a polite word for something else. I pay you to show gowns for my women customers, not to make the bedroom eyes at the men who come with them. Always, from the day you came here to work, I see you are like that. I watch, I see. And I *warned* you. I kept you on because you are a good model. The beautiful figure you undoubtedly have. But *here* you do not sell your figure. You should go on the streets if you want to do that. Here you sell my gowns."

"Well," Kathy reminded her, "the old cat bought the white and gold evening gown I showed. Two hundred and seventy-five bucks, and two hundred of it clear profit for you. That ought to please even your greedy soul, Yvette." Her own proud, defiant little soul was getting quite a lot of fun out of telling Yvette off for once. Being fired was rather pleasant in one way. You could speak your mind freely.

"It wasn't until you made me show the black and white swim suit," she added, grinning, "that all hell burst loose."

Standing before the mirror, her movements were leisurely as she perched her red beret at a provocative angle over her satiny, sleekly black hair. It was a cheap little model which she had purchased somewhere for seventy-nine cents. But Kathy gave it a fillip and the effect was sheer magic.

Or perhaps the magic was wrought by Kathy's vivid coloring. The bright flash of her smile, her upper lip sensitive and beautifully curved, the lower lip full and wide and passionate. And of course, there were her eyes…. Dark eyes, nearly black. Glowing and lively with the quick play of emotion. And perfectly enormous in her small, heart-shaped face.

She laughed softly. "It was that swim suit which started old Charley Whittaker ogling. Gosh, he was funny. I thought his eyes were going to pop right out of his head."

Madame's anger was still mounting and Kathy's casual enjoyment of the siituation was doing nothing to calm her down. "What man's eyes wouldn't have popped! Men are men. I don't suppose I need to remind *you* of that little fact. And the way you were flaunting yourself in front of him, so he couldn't miss anything you had. I was watching. I *saw*. It wasn't my suit you were showing. It was yourself."

Kathy shrugged, opening her bag to find her lipstick. "Well, my goodness," she protested, with a great pretense of injured innocence. "You want me to show your stuff to the best advantage, don't you? If you don't want your models to put a little life into the showing, why not just stick your stuff up on a stick? And anyway, the old brother seemed to be having such a nice time for himself. And he *is* sort of pathetic-looking, for all of his money. So I thought it was doing a charitable act if I could make him a little happy while I was passing his way."

"You're a shameless little slut, that's what you are." Yvette's eyes narrowed shinily. "I've a great notion to slap your face for you."

"I wouldn't," Kathy said sweetly. "You know what happened to that triple-breasted cow of a Whittaker woman when she called me an unpleasant name and then tried to trip me. I'll bet she'll be a long time forgetting that kick I gave her. *My* only regret," Kathy added thoughtfully, "is that she wasn't standing so that I could have planted my foot where it would have done more good."

She picked up her gloves and bag and turned away from the mirror, and the smile she gave Yvette was actually friendly. "Look," she said, "I'm not blaming you for firing me. I have it coming. I know I had no business brawling with one of your wealthy customers. The temptation was just too great to resist. But come down off your high horse and admit that the old sister had it coming. She is a revolting old mess, isn't she? For all of her diamonds and furs and original models, she looks more like a blown up frog than anything else I can think of."

For a second Yvette actually seemed about to break down and grin. This temptation she overcame. "Where would my business be if it were not for the unshapely old cows?" she demanded practically. "My concern is not with how they look, but with how their bank accounts look. Etta Whit-taker's account looks very good indeed. And you—you brazen, hip-twitching, impudent little fool you drive that account right out of my shop. The woman will never again set foot—"

Kathy put in comfortingly: "But Papa Whittaker must have a girl friend, wouldn't you think? So the Whittaker account may come back in through a side door. Who knows? Papa was certainly taken with that black and white swim suit. It wouldn't surprise me a bit if he'd come back and buy it for a sweetie. Plus a lot of other expensive odds and ends."

That was as it might be, Yvette said coldly. A mistress, she agreed, was sometimes a more lucrative customer than a wife. However, a wife in the hand was better than half a dozen mistresses in the bush.

"Oh," Kathy said flippantly, "but I doubt if Charley Whittaker goes in for such a primitive method. Not with all *his* money. I'd bet on a little penthouse apartment somewhere. Well, keep your chin up, Yvette. I do hope you don't go broke from losing the Whittaker account. I know you can't afford to do that. Because then you might lose that ever-loving, fancy-shirted gigolo you support, mightn't you?" For one solid year she'd been longing to make that crack, and this was too good an opportunity to miss.

Yvette's face turned livid. "Get out," she shrieked. "Get out. And don't ever set foot in here again."

Kathy flipped her gloves pertly in the woman's face. "And I say: Thanks for firing me. I've been sick of the damned job from the day I started in."

And so she had.

It had never been Kathy's idea, when she first came to New York from a little Midwest town, that she would spend her days modeling swanky clothes for jaded old hags.

That hadn't been the idea at all.

She had wanted to be a dancer. She was already awfully good at tap dancing and she had thought that might help her get a start. But she thought of it only as a start. Ballet dancing was what she wanted to do ultimately. Work that was really artistic expression. She had dreamed her bright, beautiful, fragile dreams about some day becoming the greatest ballet dancer in the world.

Anyway, she would be awfully good.

Some day—she could see it as clearly as anything in her dreams—she would dance on winged feet behind the footlights. She would hear thunderous applause. The critics would hail her as the New Discovery. Men, rich men, would send flowers by the ton as a tribute to her beauty and grace and genius. She could see the flowers heaped humbly and glowing at her feet on the stage. Could smell their heady scent as she held out her arms in gracious appreciation toward that vast audience which swayed a little before her in spellbound wonder.

And perhaps some one man—just to give the personal, intensely human touch—a romantic soul, more or less poor of course, but with a *soul*, a capacity for artistic appreciation which was beyond most of the others, would come night after night to watch her. Perhaps it would turn out that he had gone without meals, just to afford the tickets that would permit him to watch her loveliness and genius in motion. And always, night after night, he would send her a single white rose. And she would wonder and wonder about him. What sort of man he would prove to be, if they should ever meet, face to face, as man and woman. But in her dreams he never identified himself.... He remained anonymous. More of a symbol, really, than a man. A symbol of romance. And of an adoring world which she had brought to her feet....

From the time she was a very little girl she had dreamed such dreams. And for a long time they had been almost as important to her as the food she ate. More important, in some ways.

And then she got enough money together and she came to New York. And from then on, something seemed to happen to her dreams.

She had never lost them. Not quite. But dreams could become such weary, wan little things when they fed too long on utter discouragement.

For a time she had lived with an aunt in Brooklyn. But that hadn't gone so well. There were noisy children to cope with, mountains of dishes to be washed, not to mention her aunt's incessant stewing over the rising cost of living. Bread was going up. Milk was up. Butter was exorbitant, and even then, try and find any. And when you thought of what they had the nerve to charge you for *eggs*. Marking them *large* eggs, too. And when you got them home there wasn't a one you couldn't put in your eye.

Kathy's aunt simply couldn't imagine what was to become of poor people, the way things were going.

And Kathy couldn't imagine what was to become of her ballet ambitions, if she didn't escape from such a sordid atmosphere. She supposed that people like her aunt had to worry over such trivial, mundane matters as the cost of bread and eggs. But it was certainly a deadening atmosphere for the high, artistic soul. It seemed a little gross to her, really, to have to worry over the cost of things. To bother counting nickels and dimes.

She learned, however, that nickels and dimes did have their part in the scheme of things. However little you might want to, you simply had to pay them a certain respect.

She learned this, after she fell in with another girl, a would-be dancer like herself, who persuaded her that the only thing for her to do was move to "the Village," as the artistic crowd called it.

She would meet, so the girl told her, all sorts of marvelous people who would be a real inspiration to her. Artists, writers, sculptors, men and women who were doing great things in the artistic world. Or anyway, who were going to, *some day*....

"We sit around nights and have the most inspiring conversations," the girl said. "Everything about the life is an inspiration. You don't have to bother about what people think, because no one bothers to think anything, no matter what you do. If you're a woman and want to live with your lover, that's fine. Everyone understands. And if you're the type who doesn't want a lover, that's okay too. You're so *free*. So wonderfully, wonderfully free. All you have to do is just let yourself go and—well, develop. Develop your genius, I mean."

It sounded fine. So Kathy found her a little attic in Greenwich Village and moved in.

It was a little more expensive, of course. At her aunt's, there had been no question of rent to worry over. But as the rental agent explained to Kathy when she took the place: "What you pay for here, lady, is atmosphere. I'll admit the plumbing ain't much. And the dump could do with a little paint. But there's some prefer it unpainted, just dirty like it is; just like it was when some of the big shots used to live here. Guys like—oh, hell, I can't recall any of their names. Writers. Painters. They got to be big time after they left here. But they lived here once. And now you want to live here, so that's what you're paying for. Anyway, lady, paint is scarce, and damned expensive too, on account of the war.

And if you don't want the dump, I can rent it easy enough to somebody else."

So her life in the Village had begun. And the disappointments, too.

It seemed as if, no matter where she turned, she met disappointment and discouragement.

A famous ballet teacher told her quite frankly that if she worked and studied she might be good, but never any better than hundreds of others.

She haunted the casting offices, hoping to get into some show as a tap dancer. But her tap dancing, which had aroused such enthusiasm among the neighbors back in the small mid-western town, didn't seem to cause a ripple along Broadway.

Her figure aroused a little more enthusiasm. One man took an interested look at her, told her to forget the dancing. But if she'd be interested in a strip-tease act—Kathy slapped his big, beefy face and marched out. And that was that.

Finally came the modeling job at Yvette's. And the little lessons in penny-pinching. Because a girl had to eat. And what's more, the way it was turning out, a number of the friends she soon made in the Village had to eat also. And for some obscure reason, they began to look to Kathy to help solve this problem for them.

Such a bunch of bums I never did see, Kathy would think to herself sometimes, in her more disillusioned moments. They drink the other guy's liquor, make love to the other guy's woman, talk about the great things they are going to do some day. She never had heard so much big talk, with so little in the way of accomplishment to back it up.

And yet, in another way, she was crazy about the gang.

She loved their Saturday night parties, usually in her apartment, with her money buying the drinks, or the beer and rye bread and cheese. They would lounge around on the floor. The air would become blue with smoke. And the great artistic souls would orate about the great American novel they were going to do some day. Or the immortal symphony that was waiting to be composed. Or, quite frequently, about the injustices of an unappreciative world that expected them to go out and dig for a living.

The grubbing world stood ready to crucify them on a cross of meat, potatoes, and bread. Imagine! Expecting a man born with the soul of an artist to have to worry about earning a few paltry dollars just to feed his stomach.

But of course, they weren't above gorging themselves on one of Kathy's marvelous spaghetti dinners, for instance. They didn't see anything low in *that*.

Kathy would say to herself: If I stay on here I'll get just like the rest of them. As a great dancer, I'll be a marvelous talker. She really ought to get out. But she didn't do anything about it. And then Tommy Terry came along—and she didn't want to do anything about it.

Because from then on, for months and months, nothing, not even her dancing, mattered half so much as Tommy.

CHAPTER TWO

TOMMY WAS waiting for her when Kathy left the shop. There he was, tall and blond and better-looking than any screen actor, leaning against the building, reading a newspaper. Her heart tilted when she saw him. After six months, the very sight of him still did tricks to her blood pressure.

She said: "Hello, darling."

Tommy said: "Hi, kid."

He folded the newspaper, his movements slow with a leisurely grace. He put the paper in the side pocket of his overcoat, which called Kathy's attention to the fact that the pocket needed mending. She sort of wished Tommy would learn to do these little mending jobs for himself, instead of always depending on her.

For that matter, she wished they could do something about buying Tommy a new coat. It was October, and the biting cold weather was just ahead. The coat was threadbare in spots. Tommy was likely to catch an awful cold that might develop into pneumonia or something dreadful, if he tried to make it do for the whole winter. And he was so terribly brave about such things. Always passing them off with a laugh. "Clothes aren't important," Tommy would say. "Possessions aren't important. What do I care if I have to go around looking like a bum? Some day I'll be able to buy a thousand overcoats. Some day I'll write a play that will stand the critics on their ears. Some day I'll click. *Some day—*"

Kathy tucked her hand under his arm and smiled up at him. "You were sweet to meet me," she said. "I didn't expect you."

Tommy smiled lazily down at her. The look in his eyes was like a soft caress to her senses. Tommy had such marvelous eyes. They were long and blue and heavy-lidded, with long black lashes that plenty of women would have sold their souls for. His arm cuddled her hand, sending quick, exciting shivers through Kathy. "Didn't I say I'd meet you, kid?"

He had, of course, just before she left that morning. This being one of the periods when Tommy was extremely low on funds and was "bumming a bed off of Kathy," as he called it. From the couch in the alcove he had roused sleepily and called: "I'll meet you for lunch, kid."

But Tommy was quite a hand at forgetting promises like that.

He seemed to regard luncheon dates as something to be kept if you happened to think about it. And if it suited his convenience. Kathy never blamed him. She put it down to Tommy's artistic temperament.

They walked down the alley and round to Fifth Avenue. It was Saturday and the famous street was teeming with life. Smartly dressed women, brisk men walking with an air of grim purpose, idlers staring into shop windows, a crone who looked a thousand years old selling gardenias from a tray.

The gardenias seemed to remind Tommy of something. He stopped abruptly at the corner, got out a crumpled pack of cigarettes, stuck one in his mouth and shielded the match flame with his hand. He took a long drag. "Look, kid," he said, "How's about loaning me ten bucks?"

Kathy frowned. "Tommy, I can't. I just can't I—well, I just lost my job."

"You what?"

"I lost my job." And she started to giggle. "I kicked our wealthiest customer in the shins, in addition to calling her a few choice names which I lifted from your latest play. So—" she shrugged indifferently—"Yvette gave me the boot. I'm not worried. I can get another job easy enough, I guess. But until I do—well, some serious penny-pinching is indicated."

She recounted a few of the more racy details of the Whittaker episode. She had expected Tommy to be as amused as she was. After all, it really was funny. She was perfectly astounded when Tommy seemed to miss the humor in the situation. Instead, he seemed quite put out, actually annoyed with her. Kathy didn't get it. She didn't even get it—at first—when Tommy said: "I don't think you've used your head on this job. I've thought that for a long time."

Kathy's hair-line dark brow arched. "Meaning?"

"Can't you figure it for yourself, kid? Plenty of big money walks into Yvette's shop. Guys with their wives, or their girl friends. The dames look at the clothes you model, but the guys look at you. Take this Whittaker guy today. You were modeling bathing suits. By the way, how come you model swim suits in October?"

Kathy grinned. "Mrs. Money-bags is getting a few little rags together for her winter in Florida."

"Well, there's what I mean. There's precisely what I mean. The old dame is heading for Florida. The old guy will be rattling around the big town, alone. And he was giving your curves the once-over.... "

Tommy's long, lazy eyes flicked across Kathy's beautifully planned figure, just as the glances of ten out of every ten men who passed that Fifth Avenue corner were doing.

Kathy was wearing a severely plain black wool suit, belted in red the shade of her beret. The suit, and Kathy wasn't ashamed of it, had come from a second-hand shop. Which was just one of the ways she had learned to cut financial corners, and she was a little proud of it. She would even brag: "Aren't I smart? Just look what I found for a buck and a half."

If you knew the right places to go, you could pick up expensive lines and good materials for a song. Then, if you were clever with a needle—and Kathy was—you could come up with a miracle. The black outfit she wore today was a miracle. On her it was. The soft wool of the jacket hugged snugly her full, high young breasts. The short skirt was a swinging line of perfection outlining her long, beautiful legs.

"Just look at you," Tommy said. "Hasn't been a guy passed since we've been standing here who's missed that figure. And not a dame who's outclassed you."

"You like my figure, Tommy?" Kathy's dark eyes smiled at him provocatively. Her white teeth flashed. "You like my looks better than the looks of any of those fancy dames who make a play for you?"

"Not a one of them can touch you," Tommy said. But his tone was more practical than ardent. He returned to his original thesis. "Sure, you've got everything. Curves, lines, and—" he grinned a trifle—"even a face that isn't hard to take. But you don't make anything of it."

Kathy looked puzzled. "How do you mean—I don't make anything of it?"

"Well, here's what I mean, kid. Believe me, if I was a girl and had what you've got, I'd figure ways to get some gravy out of it. Believe me I would. What do you do? You've slaved at this modeling job, and all you've got out of if is that measly salary that tight-fisted witch paid you. You take dancing lessons, you practice dancing until you're half dead, you dream about becoming a great dancer. And maybe you will. But then again, maybe you won't."

"You dream about becoming a great playwright," Kathy put in. "You don't think that's silly." She added tartly: "You don't even work at anything. About all you do is dream."

"Well, that's different," Tommy said as if from some remote heights. "I'm different." But he did not explain what the difference was. "And anyway—" his eyes grew shrewd—"all the time I'm hunting around for the smart angles to play. That's what you ought to do, kid. You ought to look up some new angles, smart ones. You ought to be doing something more constructive than just working and dreaming and hanging around with a guy like me."

Kathy's eyes widened in astonishment. "Tommy Terry! What are you saying? You don't *want* me to hang around with you?" She choked back a sudden, frightening lump in her throat. "Are you telling me to get another fellow? Are you telling me you're tired of me?"

Her eyes clung to his face and suddenly there was anger in them. Kathy's quick temper was readying itself to move into high. "What is this? The old brush off?"

"No. *No*. Of course not. Don't be silly, honey." Tommy's voice was quickly soothing. He caught her arm. "Let's walk along," he said. "People are staring."

As indeed they were. It looked like a lovers' quarrel. That tall, handsome boy in the shabby coat. The small, dark girl, vivid as fire, her enormous eyes flashing angrily at him. Sure, people were staring. People were smiling. Two beautiful young people in love. They must be in love. There were a few tears mixed with the girl's hot anger. No girl could be so angry at a man unless she loved him.

They walked along slowly, heading toward Forty-second Street. "All I'm saying, if you were smart you'd play a couple of the practical angles. You got to be practical, kid. Now you take the way I am about you. I'm nuts about you. You know that, kid. You're the only dame I give a whoop about. I've told you that, haven't I?"

"Sure, Tommy. You've told me."

"And I mean it. I swear to heaven, I mean every word of it. You believe me, don't you?"

"I suppose so," Kathy said tonelessly. "Sure. I suppose you mean it. Only sometimes you've got a funny way of showing it. Every time some wealthy, middle-aged dame takes a yen for you, crooks her finger in your direction, you're off like a kite. Now you start telling me to go after another man."

"I did not tell you to go after another man. I never said anything of the sort, Dammit, you know I didn't say that."

"Maybe I don't understand English, Tommy. Maybe I'm just dumb."

"You're dumb, all right. You're just plain cuckoo, imagining any of those middle-aged, man-hungry neurotics mean a damn to me." And Tommy laughed. "But there's just what I mean when I say you ought to play a couple of other angles. That's what I'm doing. I'm playing the other angles. Hell, you don't think I *want* any of those screwball dames, do you? You don't think I'd enjoy making love to them?"

"I've heard it can be very enjoyable, that sort of thing," Kathy said. "I've heard that middle-aged women who are bored with their husbands make awfully good lovers. I've often heard people say that."

"Well, you heard it all wrong. As far as I'm concerned, there's nothing to it. Believe me, I'd never make love to any fortyish hag from choice. Believe me, kid, if I had my choice, you're all I'd ever want. And some day—some day when I've got my stuff across and am in the money—that's the way it will be. But for the present—well, I've got to be practical. I've got to think ahead."

"Were you thinking ahead yesterday," Kathy inquired sweetly, "when you broke a date with me to have cocktails with that Park Avenue female?"

She had been awfully sore at Tommy yesterday evening, and when he wandered home to the Village around nine-thirty, they had had a terrible row about it. But by mid-night Kathy had been ready to kiss and make up. She was always like that. Little spitfire that she was, her anger always burned itself out quickly because of its violence. Anyway, it was impossible to stay angry at Tommy for very long. She loved him too much.

Tommy said stiffly: "If you mean Eunice Cairn—yes. That's just what I was doing: thinking ahead. And I do wish you'd stop being so emotional and try to look at these matters sensibly."

Quite suddenly Kathy stopped, right in the middle of the pavement, and stamped a furious, red-shod foot. "Sensible! You've got a heluva nerve, Tommy Terry. Telling me in one breath you love me, and in the next, that I should take this philandering you do with a lot of fancy dames who like to have a good-looking boy fluttering around them—telling me I should take it and *like* it. For two cents, I'd call everything off between us. That's what I ought to do. If I had any pride I'd do it. I'd tell you to take that Park Avenue wench and go to blazes."

"Honey, please." Tommy caught her arm, looking worriedly around as he did so. If there was one thing Tommy couldn't stand it was a scene. It was the darndest thing about women. They'd just cut loose and make a scene anywhere, whenever the notion happened to strike them. "Psshh. Kathy, please. For Pete's sake, pipe down. Do you want all of Fifth Avenue to know our business?"

"I don't care who knows. And don't pshhh me." Suddenly she was crying. Which made her furious at herself. When she was angry enough, Kathy would invariably start crying. She detested herself for it. You lost all your dignity when you started to bawl like some fool baby.

She allowed Tommy to take her arm, to coax her along down the avenue. "If you'd only listen to what I'm trying to tell you," Tommy was saying. "Now about Eunice Cairn—there's a woman with money and influence. And I mean plenty of both. And—well, she's terribly interested in struggling young artists. Particularly writers. She makes a hobby of them, I might say."

"But they have to be tall, blond, and handsome—and strictly male, I presume?" Kathy put in acidly.

Tommy grinned, patting her hand. "Well, maybe. Oh, I'll grant you, kid, she's something of a fool. Her kind always are. But why the heck shouldn't I make the most of it? If I could get her interested enough, she might put up the dough to produce one of my plays. And then I'd be set. We'd both be set. Don't you see, kid? That's why I'm playing up to the old gal. Only yesterday I was talking with her about a couple of my plays. And she's interested. There isn't a question but what she's interested. I'm to take one up to read to her."

"But, Tommy—" a little frown worried Kathy's forehead— "you've never finished a play. You never get farther than the first act, and then you lose interest. Say she *was* willing to stake you— you'd have to get a play finished before it could be produced. Sometimes it seems to me if you'd work a little harder, if you'd stick to one of your ideas until you'd finished it up—"

"I'll get one finished," Tommy announced airily. "That's the least of my worries. I've got the stuff. I know what I'm doing. The big thing I need is somebody with some real cash who is willing to gamble on me. *But,*" said Tommy worriedly, "if a guy wants to play up to a dame like Eunice Cairn, he can't act like too much of a bum. I don't want her to think I'm just a down-at-the-heels tramp. That's why I wanted to borrow that ten bucks from you."

Kathy's dark eyes flashed a question and Tommy explained that Eunice had invited him up for cocktails that afternoon.

"Seems to be getting to be a habit," Kathy said wryly.

"Well," said Tommy, "I have to move fast, while she's interested. And of course, it was her suggestion, not mine."

"Of *course*." And Kathy laughed. But her laughter was flat, her tone scornful. "Of course. It's always the women who do the thinking and the arranging for these little twosomes you have with them. By the way, darling, what happens after you have the cocktails? Speaking of angles, that's one angle I've wondered about."

Tommy laughed blithely. "Oh, I just kid them along a little. Fading lovelies of forty or so have to be kidded, you know. That's what they thrive on. And then it's time for their ever-loving hubbies to come home from the marts of trade. So I do my I-kiss-your-hand-madame act, then the graceful fadeout."

"I see," Kathy said. But there were a number of things she didn't see at all. And one of them was the reason for the ten dollars he had wanted to bum off of her. He still hadn't explained that.

"I wanted to buy some flowers," Tommy said shortly, "if you must know. I go up there to her apartment, drink up her liquor, take up her time. I'd like to make some little gesture. Naturally, she knows I haven't any real cash. But I don't want the dame to think I'm down to my last dime."

"But you are, Tommy," Kathy reminded him practically. "I've been staking you to meals for weeks. You haven't any money for rent. All you do is talk about how broke you are. So why—"

"Do you expect me to advertise it to the world?" Tommy said sulkily. She could see his quick resentment, the flash of irritation which leaped from his mind to his eyes. He looked at her, and for a second his eyes seemed to hate her. "Do you want me to wear a placard announcing to the world that I'm broke?"

"But you don't have to be, Tommy. You could get a job like other people and then you'd have some money."

"I have my plays to write," Tommy reminded her with a touch of arrogance. "If I had wanted to plug away at some dull job, I'd have stayed back in Maryland in my dad's factory. If I had been thinking of a *salary*—" he spoke the word with a kind of fierce contempt—"I'd have stayed where I was, worked up to be vice-president, and spent my life messing over books and figures and running to the gents' toilet ever so often to break the monotony. I didn't want that. I still don't want it. I'll be damned if I'll distract my mind and destroy my talent, all for the sake of earning a few paltry dollars!"

It was quite a little speech, and it was a speech which Tommy made frequently. Kathy had heard it many times before, with variations. And she quite sympathized with his viewpoint. It was the general Village attitude—among her circle of friends, that is—toward the sordid business of slaving your life away at humdrum work, all to make a little money to live on. A disgusting business, really—this matter of needing money to exist, to eat and sleep and dress.

But now Kathy couldn't resist reminding Tommy that he shouldn't expect to have it both ways.

"If you don't want to work and have money," she told him, "you really can't expect to go around sending expensive flowers to ladies who have a yen to seduce you. Or you them," she added maliciously, "whichever way it is."

Tommy ignored that dig. "I don't expect to make a practice of it," he said stiffly. "But I would like to make the gesture. After all, it's to my advantage to get on the right side of this dame.

So I want to make a good impression. I want her to know that I understand a few of the social graces, that I'm not just a lout."

"Maybe she prefers louts," Kathy suggested sweetly. "Her kind often does. Anyway, I can't loan you ten dollars for flowers, Tommy. And that's that. Until I get another job, I've got to watch every dime, or neither one of us will eat. You wouldn't like that, would you?"

Tommy seemed peeved, thoroughly disgruntled. They had reached the corner of Forty-second Street and they stopped there, waiting for the traffic signal to change. Tommy said sulkily: "You wouldn't be so short on cash, and you wouldn't need to worry so about your next job, if you'd use your head a little. That guy today—that Whittaker guy—I know who he is. Everybody has heard of Charley Whittaker, the banker. He's rolling in dough, and no doubt has an eye out for a pretty ankle. Instead of getting into a fight with his wife, if you'd given him the wink, let him know you wouldn't be averse to him buying you a drink—"

Anger swept over her again, a seething, blinding wave that seemed almost to engulf her.

The traffic signal changed but Kathy didn't notice it. She didn't budge. "What are you saying, Tommy? Exactly what? That I should have an affair with some rich old guy so as to get money out of him? So I'd have some easy cash to loan *you*, to buy posies for your middle-aged mistress?" Her eyes flashed pinpoints of hatred at him. For a moment she actually did hate Tommy. She saw, in a quick, astounding flash, the ugly thing he was trying to do to her. Saw him for what he was as she had never seen before. The flash of clarity would pass, and with it her fleeting hatred for him. But she would never feel quite the same toward him. Not ever again.

Tommy, sensing that he had gone too far, was trying to make amends. His voice was tender, cajoling. His eyes caressing.

Tommy knew his technique with women. He knew how to treat Kathy. The kid was crazy about him. He hadn't any doubts about that. He should be careful of talking out of turn, of course. There was always that flare-up temper of hers to deal with. She was so quick to fly off the handle. Misinterpreting what he said, and how he meant it. He really should handle her more tactfully. In the future he would have to remember to do it. He hated quarrels. And when you got into a row with Kathy, it was tough going while it lasted.

But, fortunately, he always knew how to get around her. She melted like butter in the sun when he looked at her in that certain way, when he took her in his arms....

But unfortunately, this was Saturday noon, at the corner of Forty-second Street. Not the time or place, certainly, to take an angry gal in your arms.

Tommy began: "Now look, kid, you've got me all wrong. Good heavens, I don't want you to have an *affair* with any other man. That wasn't what I meant. And she's *not* my mistress. How often must I tell you? I'm only kidding the old tootsie along. There's nothing to it, absolutely nothing."

But Kathy wasn't listening. Kathy was on her way back up Fifth Avenue, alone.

CHAPTER THREE

Kathy tore along the avenue at almost a gallop.

The more she thought, the angrier she became. And the angrier she became, the faster she walked. Just imagine her standing for talk like that from any guy. "If you'd given the old guy the wink, and let him buy you a drink—"

It was all very well for other people to insist that a well-heeled boy friend could be quite an asset. But for Tommy to say it—She was simply seething with rage at Tommy. And also at herself, because she couldn't hate Tommy. She loved him too much.

Maybe it isn't love, she told herself scornfully. Maybe it's just a form of insanity.

She thought of all she had done for Tommy. Spending her own hard-earned dough to buy nice steaks and chops for him. Slaving, when she was already dog-tired, to fix meals for him that would be dainty and appetizing as well as nourishing. Because, left to himself, Tommy would doubtless live on coffee, cigarettes, and the drinks he could cadge off other people.

Buying hand-me-down clothes for herself, so that she could afford the one decent suit that Tommy owned. Calling it a birthday gift. And what did he do when he got the suit? Griped because he didn't have a decent tie and shoes to go with it. And when she came up with these accessories—laughingly calling them a present for his twenty-three years and two weeks anniversary—what then?

Well, then Tommy dolled himself up, vain as a woman about how nifty he looked, and trotted off to make a play for one of those man-hungry middle-agers who were forever going into a high fever over him.

There were times when Kathy had a few small stirring doubts about Tommy's genius as a playwright. But there was no question but that he was a champ when it came to titil-lating bored wives, ladies with big diamonds, expensive hair-rinses, and a yen for a good-looking young gigolo.

Kathy tried to take it and like it. She tried to laugh it off. Sometimes she got sore, of course. Sometimes, just thinking about it, she got so furious she couldn't see straight. As now ...

She suddenly plunged head-on, square into the man who was coming her way.

There was no way for him to avoid the collision. She was coming at him like such a streak of lightning. So he simply caught both her arms, bringing both of them to an abrupt stop.

And then he took another look at her and said: "Well, if it isn't the little model—"

Kathy looked up at him, apologizing quickly for getting in his road. She laughed. "I guess I wasn't looking where I was going." Then: "Oh, it's *you*, Mr. Whittaker."

He smiled. "Yes. It's me."

He was a small man, of around fifty, and somehow he reminded Kathy of a little brown robin. His tired eyes were about the same shade of brown as his overcoat and tie. He wore gold-rimmed spectacles and he was very neat. He seemed nice, too. He had a nice smile and a nice voice. And he was the kind of man you never would have looked at twice, unless you had practically run over him, as Kathy had. You never would have guessed, to look at him, that he was Charley Whittaker, one of New York's wealthy bankers.

And you never would have dreamed that behind that mouselike exterior, there breathed the soul of an adventurous romanticist.

Kathy said: "Well, I do hope you'll forgive me for almost knocking you down. I—I had something on my mind."

"That's all right," Mr. Whittaker said. He smiled. "I often do the same thing myself. I get to day-dreaming when I'm walking along, and I forget there's anyone else on the street." And then he added: "I'm really glad it happened. It gives me a chance to apologize for my wife's—well, shall we say, thoughtlessness?" He looked embarrassed. "She said some unkind things to you, I'm afraid. I hope you'll overlook it. Unfortunately, Mrs. Whittaker has rather a quick tongue."

Kathy grinned. "Oh, that's all right. I suppose I asked for it. I did kick her, you know. I shouldn't have done that, but she made me so sore—accusing me of flirting with you, and right before half a dozen other customers." She laughed roguishly. "A model is supposed to do a little swaying and hip-swinging, you know, to show off the garments to the best advantage. I was only working at my job. I wasn't trying to make a play for you."

"Of course you weren't," said Mr. Whittaker in his mild, pleasant voice. "No one ever makes a play for me." And if there was regret in his tone he covered it with a smile. "But Etta always imagines they do. She's a very jealous woman—extremely jealous." He sighed. "There's very little a man can do about a woman who gets jealous over nothing at all. I certainly hope her unpleasant outburst caused you no embarrassment."

"Oh, no," Kathy said cheerfully. "It only cost me my job, that's all."

"Oh, my goodness. That won't do." Mr. Whittaker seemed not only shocked but really distressed. He looked at her earnestly. "Do you really mean to tell me—"

Kathy nodded. "Yvette fired me. But don't worry. I can find another job. And I had it coming. I know the rules. A model doesn't talk back to the customers, no matter what." She grinned.

"And she *certainly* doesn't go around kicking Mrs. Charley Whittaker in the shins." She smiled. "It's nice of you to be concerned about me. But don't worry. There's no great harm done." And she started to walk on, never expecting the man to turn and fit his pace to hers.

"See here." He caught her arm. "We can't let it go at this, you know. There's been an injustice done. And I feel that I'm to blame."

"You?" Kathy gave him her sweetest smile. He was rather a dear. And he actually did seemed worried about her. "Why, don't be silly. You to blame! You didn't do a thing."

"But I did," he insisted gravely. And then unexpectedly, as he looked at her, there was a really lively twinkle in those tired brown eyes. "I *looked*, you know. I really did look. Mrs. Whittaker was quite right to say I was—just how did she put it?"

"Ogling," Kathy giggled. "She said, 'Charley, stop ogling the little tart.'"

"So she did," Charley said, flushing with faint embarrassment. But the twinkle still livened his eyes, and his hand on her arm pressed a little more insistently. "She shouldn't have called you that, of course. But I was ogling," he insisted. "You're quite something to look at, you know, Miss—Miss—"

"Neilson," Kathy supplied. "Kathy Neilson."

"Well, Kathy, you're exceptionally pretty. And in that black and white bathing suit—my, my—" He shook his head. "I doubt if I ever saw a prettier figure, even on the stage. I just couldn't take my eyes off of you. But you mustn't hold that against me, my dear." And his fingers squeezed her arm playfully. "You wouldn't blame an old fellow like me for looking, would you?"

"Naturally not!" Kathy drawled, slanting her eyes at him provocatively. "My goodness, it seems to me that any man is entitled to *look*."

This seemed to tickle him. He laughed delightedly, at the same time getting a firmer grip on her arm. "You're cute," he said. "You're awfully cute."

"So I've been told," Kathy retorted flippantly. Then, as they came to a corner, she stopped abruptly. She had been racking her brains to figure how to get rid of him without being rude. Wealthy bankers, she was deciding, weren't very different from other men. They stuck like glue, if they liked your curves. She was very pleased that the wealthy Charley Whittaker liked her figure. It was quite bolstering to her ego. Because a man like that must have been around. He must know a good figure when he saw one.

But just the same she wanted to get rid of the guy.

She had nothing to say to him and she had her own troubles to think about. He was such a quaint little man. And, crazy as it sounded, he struck her as being lonely.

Well, Kathy knew her lonely men. Charley might try to engineer her into a cocktail bar somewhere, and keep her stuck there while he talked and talked and talked. So Kathy stopped at the corner and said, pleasantly enough: "Look, Mr. Whittaker, it's been nice having this little talk with you and all. But now I'm afraid I'll have to be running on, alone. I've a lot of shopping to do."

"Shopping?" This seemed to interest him. He looked at her archly. "Well, now, how about my coming along with you? I've always thought I'd like to help a pretty girl do her shopping."

Kathy gave him a naughty wink. "Now, now, Mr. Whittaker—"

"I wish you'd call me Charley," he said unexpectedly. "It would seem more friendly."

"Okay, Charley. And what I started to say—I'm not going shopping for what *you* think." She grinned. "I'm not a glamour girl, you know. So I can't afford expensive undies."

Had she wanted to be quite honest about it, she would have said: I can't afford undies. Period.

This caused her companion to inquire interestedly how she spent her time when she wasn't on the job as a model. And when Kathy told him that she had ambitions to become a dancer, that she lived in a Greenwich Village attic, the little man became quite excited.

"Is that a fact?" he said. "So you're ambitious to be a dancer. And you live in the Village. I suppose there's quite a colony of artists living there." He seemed to regard her with new interest.

"There's quite a colony of would-be artists," Kathy said with a wry grin. "No one I know seems to be getting anywhere as yet. We're mostly *some day* big shots."

"I see," Charley said. He kept looking at her. "I suppose there are some writers, along with the others. And you probably live quite a gay, Bohemian life. It must be very fascinating."

There was a queer longing in his voice, which Kathy did not detect for what it was. She was quite accustomed to people thinking you were terribly Bohemian, and somehow to be envied, the minute they heard you lived in the Village. As often as not, of course, they looked at you with severe disapproval, as much as to say: *Well,* you can't tell me anything about that Village crowd. Drinking, carousing, maybe taking dope, and no morals at all. That's life in the Village. And there was no use at all in telling them that for the most part, these days, the Village was occupied by the most commonplace, everyday sort of people. Clerks and such who moved there because it was the cheapest place they could find to live, and still be near the heart of the city.

There was no use in telling them because they wouldn't believe you. They would go right on regarding you as an unmoral hussy.

But just the same the envy was there, mixed in with the disapproval. There was somehow something glamorous attached to life in Greenwich Village. The mark of high romance. The touch of adventurous living. It branded you as one of those who dared to live more deeply and dangerously than lesser souls.

When Kathy noticed the touch of envy in Charley Whittaker's voice, she was faintly amused. She had no way of knowing that quiet, reserved Charley, with his sly arm-pinching, was a high romanticist at heart. And that once, long ago—before his banker father had set his foot down on such foolishness and insisted that Charley get down to the serious business of work behind a little cage-window—Charley had dreamed his own pretty dreams about becoming a famous writer.

She had no way of knowing that even now, in his spare time, Charley amused himself writing adventure stories which he sent around to the pulp magazines under an assumed name, and which were promptly returned to the post office box which he rented for that purpose.

Charley said now: "Well, this is certainly most interesting. I've often wished I knew someone who lived in the Village. I'd like to come and see you sometime. Would that be all right?"

"Oh, sure," Kathy said carelessly. "We keep open house. Anyone is welcome." She grinned. "Even wealthy bankers. And now I've really got to get to my shopping."

"Oh, yes. About your shopping. If it isn't too impertinent, would you mind telling me what you were going to buy?"

"A winter coat," Kathy lied, because it was the first thing that came to her mind. "I need a new coat before the cold weather sets in."

This information gave Charley another idea. "Well, now," he said, "that's fine. Of course you need a new coat. You must be properly protected against the cold. And since you're such a pretty girl, you should have a very pretty coat. Now, how about letting me buy one for you?"

Kathy stared, and her tone was sharp. Her eyes held sudden little glints. "Say," she said, "what's the idea? What kind of a gal do you take me for, Mr. Whittaker? *Do I look,*" she demanded, "like I'm the kind that walks three blocks with a guy and then lets him buy me a coat? I suppose," she added icily, "you had a snappy little mink number in mind?"

"Why, yes. If you like mink, I'd be very happy to buy you a mink coat. And please don't take this the wrong way. Nothing was farther from my mind than—well—" he smiled a trifle—"reflecting on your character. I never thought of such a thing."

"Of course not," Kathy drawled mockingly. She really was offended. And yet she couldn't honestly say there was anything offensive in his manner.

"I'd really like to buy you a gift," Charley was saying earnestly. "Look at it this way. I've caused you quite a bit of trouble today. I've cost you your job."

"Your wife did that, not you."

"Well, no matter. I feel responsible. I feel very badly about it. You're obviously a sincere, ambitious girl who's making a brave struggle to make something of yourself, and I can well understand it can't be very pleasant to be pitched out of your job for no fault of your own. I don't want to go around with it on my conscience that I let that happen to you and did nothing to make amends. I really must do something for you, Kathy. And if a mink coat would please you, it would give me a great deal of pleasure to buy it for you."

"Well, thanks awfully. But I couldn't let you do it. Why—" she giggled suddenly—"if I went back to the Village sporting a mink coat, I'd be ostracized. They'd say I was a kept woman."

He smiled a trifle. "And your friends in the Village wouldn't approve of that?"

"Definitely not." She rounded her eyes in mock gravity. "In the Village, the gals support the boy friends. But the other way round—that simply isn't done, my friend." She laughed and held out her hand.

"Thanks for the nice gesture, Charley. You meant well and I appreciate it. But I don't belong to the mink coat sister-hood. Anyway, not yet."

He took her hand and he didn't seem to want to let it go. He held on and held on. And he looked so worried. "But I must do something for you," he said earnestly. "Is there anything you can think of that you'd like, and that you would accept?"

"Oh, sure." And just to kid him along Kathy gave his hand a nice warm squeeze.

This seemed to excite him. "You're so sweet," he said. "You're just the sweetest little thing. You do like me a little, don't you, Kathy?"

"Of course. I think you're an old dear."

"I'm not so very old," he said defensively. "I'm not as old as I probably look. Why," he added more vigorously, "plenty of men ten, twenty years older than I am have married girls no older than you, and had strong, healthy children by them, too."

"They must have been some men." Kathy couldn't resist grinning.

"I'm not as old as you think," he repeated stubbornly. "How old do you take me to be?"

Kathy looked him over thoughtfully, pretending to consider the question with profound seriousness. Finally: "Well, I'll tell you. I think you're still young enough for Mrs. Whittaker to keep an eye on. But you're too old to go tossing mink coats at the first cute little model who wiggles an eye at you." She freed her hand at last and shook a reproving finger at him.

"You're old enough to know better than that, Charley."

Charley purred: "You darling." He looked quite arch. He seemed delighted with the way she had expressed it. He caught her hand back. "Maybe I'm old enough to know better," he said shamelessly, but I'm not too old to want to."

Then he remembered something. "You were going to tell me what I could give you."

"Oh, yes." Kathy grinned. 'Well, bring me a steak. A nice, thick, juicy one."

"A steak?" He smiled. "You're kidding me, Kathy."

"I am *not*. Kidding, he sez. Charley, you're behind the times, way behind. I can see that you rich bankers don't keep up with this brave new world we're supposed to be living in."

She patted his arm with a maternal gesture. Then, impishly, she leaned close and whispered in his ear. "In the old days, the gals held out for furs, diamonds, and silk lingerie. But no more. Now we give the key to the boudoir to the lad who comes up with thick red meat."

His laugh was coy. "Are you offering me a key?"

"I might think about it," she retorted teasingly.

She flashed him a white smile. "I'd *think* about practically *anything*—in exchange for a steak."

CHAPTER FOUR

HERE was a girl seated on the pavement with her easel when Kathy reached the shabby old Macdougal Street house. Kathy said: "Hi, Babs," and stopped a moment. "How's the painting going?"

"Lousy," the girl said. She was thin, hollow-chested, with a pallor that made her look almost wraith-like. She wore a drooping black velvet beret over her blonde hair and a green smock.

"How's Fred?"

"*That* drunken, no-good so-and-so." Babs' voice sounded a little hysterical. "That skunk. I should never have married him."

There was some question as to whether Babs and Fred ever had actually married, but Kathy was polite enough not to mention it. She felt awfully sorry for Babs. Fred wasn't any good. He spent half of his life lying around drunk. Occasionally, just to vary the monotony, he would beat Babs up and Babs would run around displaying her bruises, threatening to kill Fred. Or herself. Or maybe both of them. And then the next thing you knew, Fred and Babs would be making hectic love to each other.

This was one of the days when Babs was carrying a honey of a bruise. She jerked up the wide sleeve of her smock, baring her shoulder. "Look at that," she said. "Just *look*. Why do I stand for it? Kath, I'm going to kill myself. I've thought it all out and I'm going to find a way out of the whole rotten mess. Why shouldn't I kill myself?" Her voice calmed for the first time.

Kathy looked at the bruise. It was purplish, an angry welt. She patted Babs' thin arm. "You should put some ointment on that. And I think you'd be pretty silly to kill yourself."

"Why? Tell me why!"

"Well, Fred isn't worth it, that's why. Why don't you kick the heel out? Forget him. Then go on with your painting. Do some good, hard work at it."

"Paint! How can I paint! How can I create, when my heart is breaking?"

The worst of it was that Babs was extremely talented.

When she first came to New York, before Fred had got his deadly hold on her, she had had two or three character studies on display at a gallery exhibit. One had won a prize. Lately, however, her work had gone all to pieces.

"You're a worse fool than I take you for," Kathy said practically, "if you break your heart over that phony. Get wise to yourself, honey. Fred is nothing but a drunken bum. That's all he'll ever be. So what's the point in eating your heart out over him? Not to mention wrecking your life."

This remark seemed to rub Babs the wrong way. "You're a fine one to be calling *my* man a bum," she snapped, "after the way you let Tommy Terry play you for a sucker. I'll say this much for Fred, he isn't a gigolo. He may get tight and beat me up. But he doesn't run around town, making a play for any rich, middle-aged dame who happens to take a yen for his physique."

Kathy had to smile. That was Babs for you. One minute Fred was a brutal heel. The next, she was ready to fly like a wildcat to his defense. Kathy shrugged for a moment and went on up the steps.

She paused for a moment before she opened the door, looking back down the street. This was the famous Village. A narrow street, dirty, ugly, the houses old and run down. It was supposed to have glamour. And the funny part was that it had. The little basement shops were cheap and smelly. Trash scurried about the gutters. The most commonplace-looking people passed up and down. And yet—was it that ghosts walked there? The ghosts of those who had once struggled there, before they shot up to fame? O. Henry, for instance. An emaciated girl passed in a shabby coat with a motheaten fur collar. And you thought of O. Henry.... It was of such as she that O. Henry had written. He had seen the drama and the human yearnings and the dreams, and the stubborn pride behind the shabby little people with their lonely, hungry eyes. And he had written stories about them that would never die.

Maybe that was the intangible something that refused to die, and why the charm of the Village lived on. You might not be able to see the high human drama behind the sordid shabbiness of the narrow, alley-like streets. But you felt it. You felt it in your heart.

Kathy opened the door and went into a dismal narrow hall with ancient paper peeling off the walls. The odor of cabbage cooking came to her unpleasantly. She walked up uncarpeted stairs to the third floor and was starting up the last flight to her attic apartment when a door opened and a flushed, disheveled little man appeared. He was smoking a cigarette and his thinning hair seemed to stand on end.

"Miss Neilson," he said in a loud whisper. "Just a minute. Just a minute, please."

Kathy smiled a "Oh, hello, Mr. Peterson." It did not surprise her that he looked terribly upset. Henry Peterson was a shoe clerk who took life very seriously and was invariably upset over something. Either his unpaid bills, or his sinus trouble. Or, as recently, because his wife was going to have a baby, her first. And Henry worried for fear lest, at thirty-six, she was too old for it.

Kathy leaned over the banister and Henry came close to it, peering up into her face. He said: "Miss Neilson, as you know my wife is in a delicate condition."

"Yes, of course. How is Mrs. Peterson?" Kathy inquired.

Henry Peterson shook his head. He seemed very jittery. His plump cheeks quivered and his nicotine-stained fingers shook as he fumbled lighting another cigarette. "Not well. Not well at all. I'm terribly worried. She seems to be all nerves. Hattie is thirty-six, you know, and I'm afraid she shouldn't have attempted this ordeal. Every little noise disturbs her. And that's why I stopped you, Miss Neilson."

The little man looked at her severely. "This is Saturday, you know."

"So it is," Kathy agreed brightly. "So what?"

"Miss Neilson, I don't like having to say this. I hope you won't take it the wrong way. I'm not one to interfere with other people having a little fun. But what goes on in your apartment on Saturday nights is not fun. It sounds more like a riot. Last Saturday night, the house simply shook with all your carrying on." His voice had risen until it was an angry little squeak.

"It lasted until five o'clock in the morning. Five o'clock, Miss Neilson. And my wife was such a wreck, I was worried it might bring on a miscarriage. I'm a tolerant man, and I'll stand for a lot. But I won't stand for a bunch of drunken Bohemians causing my wife to have a miscarriage. That I will not stand. I'm warning you."

Kathy looked startled for a moment; then she laughed. "I'm sorry if we disturbed you," she said. "But after all, it was just a little party. If you don't like to hear noisy parties, you should move out in the suburbs somewhere, Mr. Peterson. This is Greenwich Village," she reminded him, smiling. "You don't expect us to just sit around and knit, do you?"

"I don't care what you do," blustered Henry, "just so you keep quiet about it. Oh, I'm not saying I *approve* of the way some in this house carry on. I'm a religious man myself. I was brought up in a very religious family and I do not approve of promiscuous—"

"Now, now, Mr. Peterson." Kathy shook a warning finger at him. "In just a minute, you're going to say a naughty word and you'll never forgive yourself."

Henry flushed a trifle. "Well, anyway, I will not stand for all this rough-house on Saturday nights. Week nights it's bad enough. Sometimes I wonder if the floor is coming down on my head. I can't imagine what you do up there."

"I guess it's my tap dancing," Kathy said sweetly. "Wouldn't you like to come up and watch me tap dance sometime? If you watched how hard I work, maybe you'd be more sympathetic."

The suggestion seemed to leave Henry completely cold. He was not interested in tap dancing. He was interested only in his wife's delicate condition. And her nerves. And for that matter, his own nerves. "There are people in this house," he reminded her, "who have to *work* for a living. They need their sleep. My wife must have her sleep. I must have my sleep or I'll be a complete wreck. And I'm warning you for your own good, Miss Neilson. If there's a repetition of last Saturday night, I shall have to take steps. I happen to know you are behind in your rent. And if I go to the manager of this building and complain about the drunken, immoral carryings on in your room—"

"So I'm behind in the rent." Kathy laughed brightly. "Well, that's a funny one. Where did you pick up that piece of misinformation? I've never been behind in the rent. Never once."

"I've said my say," said Mr. Peterson. "I've *warned* you."

Kathy went on upstairs to her apartment, which was definitely a de luxe name for the long, slanting-roofed attic room with its bare floor and old-fashioned black stove stuck in the middle of the floor.

Some flowered cretonne at the small windows and a few cheap pictures gave it touches of color. An India print thrown over the couch where Kathy slept, with pillows strewn over it, made that one corner rather cozy-looking. But at best, it was a shabby, dismal place, viewed by conventional standards.

But of course Kathy and her gang never viewed such matters by conventional standards. They believed that the very fact that it was an attic lent atmosphere. Of course, there were only two chairs, and those straight-backed and uncomfortable. But who wanted chairs? There was a floor, wasn't there? And you could put pillows on it. The big, round, ungainly table looked as solid and as ugly as granite, but it was a swell place to climb up and do a dance when liquor gave you the urge. Or for one of the girls to pose on, when Jack Dalby had had sufficient shots to feel the inspiration for one of his charcoal nudes.

Several little alcoves were curtained off with cheap crash drapes. One of these concealed the three burner gas range and Kathy's other kitchen accessories. She went behind another to undress.

What with all the confusion in her mind, Kathy decided a little practice dancing was indicated. That was her way of working off steam when she was angry or upset. And she was still simply furious at Tommy. She thought about him a little now, as she stepped out of her dress and undies and slipped on the tight-fitting black sateen gym trunks and the very brief bra which she wore for practice work.

She just couldn't figure Tommy out. Plenty of the time he seemed to love her like crazy. And then he'd pull something, such as his talk today, which made her wonder if he had the foggiest idea what love was all about. She wondered a little, too, what that dame Eunice Cairn was like. All Kathy really knew about her was that she had a rich husband and a Park Avenue apartment and was quite a hound for the famous New York night spots. Tommy had shown Kathy a newspaper picture of Eunice taken at the Stork Club with some marine officer draping his arm around her. In the picture Eunice looked sleek and expensive and she-wolfish.

Kathy came out from behind the drapes wearing her skin-tight trunks. There was a somewhat blurred mirror on one wall which gave her a flashed reflection of herself, and Kathy grinned at what she saw. Not bad, she thought. Her dark curls were flying and her eyes were bright. She was a pretty thing and she knew it. She was pretty enough to do better for herself than hang around with a Tommy Terry. If only she had sense enough to do better....

Oh, well, she supposed a girl in love shouldn't expect to have sense. If you had a lot of sense about it, it probably wouldn't be love. And not half so much fun, either, she'd bet.

She pushed the big table out of the way to clear a spot of floor space, turned on the radio to a dance program, and for the next ten minutes or so she forgot everything but her dance practice.

A few exercises first to limber herself up. Then into her tap dancing ...

When someone knocked Kathy said, "Oh, heck," and ran to the door. A man in overalls stood there. Youngish. With impudent, interested dark eyes which became more and more interested as they looked Kathy up and down. "Hi, Toots," he said, pushing his cap to a rakish angle at the back of his head. His glance seemed to concentrate on the black bra.

Kathy looked back at him. "Fresh guy, eh?" she said. She was not greatly disturbed. Some fresh mutt was always wandering up to your door in the Village. You didn't pay him any attention. If a girl was a dancer and working at it, she certainly didn't run to get into a Mother Hubbard before she answered the door. If the guy got too smart, you slammed the door in his face. This one merely continued to stare until Kathy asked:

"What do you want, anyway? I'm busy."

"With the boy friend?" The man winked.

Kathy grinned. "If you must know, I have three sick grandmothers and five dying children in here. They're all screaming for me to bring them food. Can't you hear them screaming? Look, if you just knocked at my door because you felt lonely and wanted to make with a little conversation—"

The man held out a bill to her. "Sorry, Toots. I came on business. You're behind in your electric light bill and it's about to be turned off. I'm a regular little boy scout at heart, so I thought I'd drop by and warn you. If you can give me the dough now I can fix it up for you."

Kathy stared. "But I've paid my last bill—" And she had, too. Anyway, she had given Tommy the money to pay it. A horrible thought crossed her mind. She remembered what Mr. Peterson had said: "I happen to know you're behind in your rent."

She had also given Tommy the money to attend to *that*. She figured it saved postage and the cost of a money order if she gave him the money to take to the office direct. And she herself was never free in the daytime to attend to such matters.

Now she began to wonder. If that heel Tommy had been putting something over on her—The man said: "You haven't paid your last three bills. Too bad, beautiful. But—no money, no lightee."

"But I can't pay you now," Kathy said. "If you must know, I'm running in a spot of bad luck. I lost my job today. I need the money I have to eat on for the next few days. Anyway, I don't understand this at all. Are you sure there isn't some mistake? I gave my friend the money to take to the electric company."

"Boy friend?" the man suggested, grinning. "So it's the old story. Maybe the boy friend figured he needed a drink more than you needed your light. Or maybe you'd better check up on the guy. Could be there's a blonde in his life. Had you thought of that?"

"Oh, don't be funny," Kathy said crossly.

"Look," she said after a minute, "isn't there some way you could give me a little more time? If you can wait until the middle of next week—"

The man shook his head. "I only work for the company, beautiful. I was sent up here to check your meter and turn the juice off. I only came up to warn you out of the kindness of my heart." He thought for a moment, while his glance passed avidly over Kathy's warm, glowing, and not too securely clad young figure. "But I'll tell you what I will do. You invite me in for—well, say an hour—and I'll advance the dough for you."

Kathy scowled at him. "Will you indeed! And do you know what I'll do? You make another crack like that and I'll give you a good fast kick in the shins. I'm extremely good at shin-kicking," she added.

He grinned. "What's the use in putting on an act, beautiful? This ain't the first Greenwich Village door I've knocked at. Or the first time I've been received by a dame in her see-mores. You gals are broadminded when you want to be. And this seems a mighty good time for you to want to be, Toots. Now say you and I get together for an hour or two and who knows what it might develop into? Huh? How's about it, cutie?" And his hand came and smacked the black sateen trunks. "Boy." He gave a low whistle. "You certainly are built, aren't you, babe? They weren't fooling when they turned you out. I could sure go for you. Why, dammit, I might end up paying your electric bills on a permanent basis. And that's going pretty strong for a guy like me with two hungry babies to feed."

"Well, you'd better toddle along and feed them, brother," Kathy said, and slammed the door in his face.

CHAPTER FIVE

KATHY went back into the room, and her first act was to pick up a geranium pot and hurl it as hard as she could at the floor. She supposed she really should try to control her temper. Well, maybe she'd get around to that, when she was older. For now, it was much more satisfactory to let it simply rip into high.

If that heel Tommy had used her money instead of paying her bills with it! To send flowers to that Cairn dame, most likely. She was so furious she started to cry again. And her eyes were still wet with tears when someone else knocked. Still wearing her black trunks and bra, and quite unconscious of them, Kathy ran to the door. It was another man.

A rather engaging-looking man, this time. Not exactly handsome, but definitely striking-looking. His teeth were as white as his hair was black. His eyes were dark and lively in a face that was exceptionally well sculptured. His cheek-bones were high, his features clean cut and regular. He wore dark trousers, an immaculately white shirt, and an eye-shade. There was a pencil stuck behind his ear.

He said pleasantly: "Would you like me to dispose of the body for you?"

Kathy's eyes rounded. "I beg your pardon?"

"The body. My name's Dexter. Matt Dexter. I live right under you. That smash a minute ago—I figured you must be murdering the guy. Well, I was in the Marines until a couple of months ago. So slugging and moving dead bodies are right up my alley. I figured I'd be neighborly and offer my assistance."

"Oh. That." Kathy giggled. "That was just a flower pot. I was annoyed over something. I was just letting off a little steam."

"I see. Just having fun, eh?" The man's dark eyes studied her. Long, lean, he lounged against the door frame. He was smoking a pipe and he cupped the bowl of it in his hand. "Well, look, couldn't you try cutting paper dolls for a change? I was in the South Pacific for two years, and I've been here for two weeks. And for a nice, quiet spot where a man can concentrate, give me the foxholes any day. How do you expect a man to get any work done with the plaster shaking down around his head and—"

Kathy grinned. "You sound just like Henry Peterson. Only different, of course. He's going to have a baby, that's his trouble. You aren't going to have a baby, are you, Mr. Dexter?"

"Not that I know of. Why don't you have one?" he suggested earnestly. "Had you thought of that? It might help to quiet you down. What the hell do you do up here, anyway?" he asked. "I mean, when you're not hurling flower pots around. I never heard such a racket."

Kathy suspected that he was more in earnest than she had guessed at first, and it annoyed her vaguely. Good heavens, all this fuss about a little noise. Whatever did people expect when they moved into a Village apartment? They ought to have sense enough to know it wasn't a graveyard.

"I can't see as I make so much noise," she argued. "Oh, I admit, I do get in a bad humor sometimes—and throw things. And when my friends come in evenings, I guess we sort of forget there are neighbors around. And then, of course, there's my dancing. I'm going to be a dancer, you know."

"Really?" His dark eyes flicked over her, and for the first time Kathy was a little too self-conscious about the scantiness of her attire. "Well," he said, and he grinned a trifle, "you seem to have the figure for it. Nice," he added significantly. "Very nice."

Kathy felt her face flush red. She didn't like his tone nor his faintly mocking smile. "I wasn't referring to my figure," she reminded him tartly. "I was talking about my dancing. Just leave my figure out of it."

He shrugged. "Okay by me, sister. I've seen plenty of pretty legs in my time. I can take 'em, or leave 'em alone. Yours are pretty nice, but don't get the idea I'm the type to work up a lather over them. Although if you don't mind my mentioning it—if you don't want your callers to get an eyeful, how come you run around half naked?" His tone was as impersonal as if he were discussing the price of tomatoes.

"I was tap dancing," Kathy retorted. "Not that it's any of your business. And I might remind you that no one asked you to come calling at my door. This is *my* apartment. And as long as I pay my rent, I have a right to hurl flower vases or go around dressed this way, or anything else I choose to do. And it's none of your confounded business."

"But you haven't paid your rent," Matt Dexter said coolly. "That's just the point. That's one reason I came up, as a matter of fact. See here, Miss—by the way, what is your name?"

Kathy told him, while fear and suspicion began tugging at her. Here it was again. Someone else, another stranger, warning her that her rent wasn't paid....

"Okay, Kathy. I'm going to be frank with you. I'm just out of the war by way of a medical discharge. I have a contract to do a book on my war experiences."

"Oh," she cut in disagreeably. "Another phony writer, eh?"

His pipe had gone out and he knocked the bowl of it against the wall. He looked at her. "No," he said. "Not a phony writer. A writer who writes. A writer with a real job to do and, by heaven,

I have to have a little peace and quiet to do it in. I'm a reasonable fellow, Kathy. I'm the last one to interfere with the other fellow's fun. But I'd like a little consideration shown me, too. You and your little playmates haven't a spark of consideration for anyone but yourselves. You drink and howl up here until all hours—"

"We don't, either. And anyway—"

"You make love and you fight and you—"

"We don't mean anything by it. Honest. We're only—"

"And when you're alone, just to keep things lively, you gallop about like a wild pony, and then start throwing things."

"Kindly don't refer to my tap dancing as galloping around like a wild horse," Kathy said with sudden dignity. "And anyway, if you had any wits, you'd know you have to expect that sort of thing in the Village. Surely you know the type of people who live here."

"Mostly hard-working people who want their sleep," Matt Dexter told her severely.

"Well—" Kathy tossed her head airily—"that kind shouldn't move in here. They have no business here. The Village was intended for an artistic colony."

"Baloney. Don't hand me that artistic stuff. Next thing you'll be telling me you're only *expressing* yourself when you all but kick the floor through."

"And so we are," Kathy agreed sweetly. "That's exactly what we're doing: expressing ourselves." She had a sudden idea. "I'll bet you don't even believe I am a dancer. Well, come on in. I'll dance for you. I'll prove to you whether I'm a dancer or not."

The young man thought this over for a moment. "No," he said finally. His eyes ran over her slim, curved loveliness, the softly moving mounds of her bosom, her slender beautiful legs, and seemed to decide against yielding to whatever temptation he found in them. "No, thanks. I'm not saying you can't dance.

Even if you can't, you'd be pretty nice to watch. I wouldn't be against coming in and looking you over more carefully—" his smile was not altogether nice—"if my mind wasn't on this job I've got to do. But I'm a guy who doesn't believe in mixing work and pleasure. After I've finished a job, then I like to breeze out and find me an attractive gal and have fun. That's fine—when I haven't anything else on my mind. But you're only wasting your time, honey, trying to proposition me just now. I don't happen to be in the mood."

"I'm not trying to proposition you," Kathy said furiously. "And you—you're insulting, you big lug. You—you're just like Marines are supposed to be. You haven't any of the finer feelings."

"Nope," Matt Dexter agreed cheerfully. "That's me all right. Not a finer feeling to my name. And no particularly low feelings right now, either, if you want to know. Right now, I'm only a guy who has a job to do and wants a quiet place to do it in. That's why I stepped in to see the rental agent this morning and asked if he couldn't find me a quieter room to live in. So he suggested the place right above me. And that means yours. He tells me you're way behind in the rent and, if I want the place, he'll put you out. Don't get me altogether wrong, honey. I'm not a guy to go around putting a gal who's broke out of house and home. Dammit, I'd hate myself for doing a stunt like that. But if you force me to it, chum, I'll have to get tough."

His parting shot was delivered without even a grin. "Cut out the rough stuff, Kathy. Or else."

He walked away, and Kathy stood there, watching him go. She was both shocked and indignant and a little scared. And her mind was in too much of a whirl for her to think of a quick, defiant comeback. She noticed that he limped a trifle as he went down the narrow stairs. She noticed his proud, really beautiful dark head. She wanted to be angry at him. But her sense of fairness reminded her that there was really no logic in being angry.

She was an utter stranger to him. She was merely a girl who lived in the room over his. And, thinking it over now, she realized that neither she nor the rest of her crowd had ever given a thought to how much commotion they made, or whether other people in the house might be disturbed.

Often their parties did last until breakfast. They danced and they screamed and they whooped it up. And sometimes things became lively indeed, as when Babs and Fred staged one of their fights, and Babs started screaming about Fred being a drunken brute....

And it just never occurred to any of them that they might be disturbing other people, or to care in the least, if they did happen to think about it. Let joy be as unconfined as they darned pleased. That was the theory they went on.

It was the Village, wasn't it? So what could people expect?

Well, the rental agent expected his money on time. That was *one* thing that was expected. And it seemed pretty plain by now to Kathy that Tommy had made off with the rent money, plus the electric light money. Plus—what other money she had given him to pay bills.

She wasn't so much angry by now as just plain worried.

What in the world was she to do?

It was no longer quite so funny—having lost her job with Yvette. Oh, she could get another job, some sort of job. But it would take a little time. And meanwhile, she had nothing ahead. Just two dollars, and maybe a little change.

And she was likely to be put out of her apartment any minute.

She drew a long, difficult breath and was about to turn back into the room and close the door when a boy came trudging up the stairs with a long box. It looked like a flower box.

The kid saw her and called to her: "I got a box here for a Miss Kathy Neilson. Know where I'll find her?"

Kathy took the box and signed for it. She closed the door and carried it into the room, putting it on the heavy round table to open. She was definitely curious. Long flower boxes carrying the name of an expensive Fifth Avenue florist just didn't happen in her life. She wondered if this was some gesture on Tommy's part. If the heel had used up all her cash, and then gone out and ordered flowers for her!

It would be like him, she thought, with a quick softening of her heart toward him. Yes, it would be exactly like Tommy to have her thrown out of her apartment for non-payment of rent, and then send her expensive flowers. The sentimental idiot would be perfectly capable of doing just that. And I'd probably forgive him all, Kathy thought, knowing her own tremendous and more or less insane weakness where Tommy was concerned.

Only the flowers were not from Tommy.

She cut the silvered ribbon and opened the box.

A dozen long-stemmed roses lay, blood red and moistly lovely, in their long tissue cradle.

She lifted them out carefully, one by one. They were the loveliest flowers she had ever had. She thought worriedly: I haven't a vase large enough to put them in without cutting the stems. Maybe Lucille Moffat could loan her something. Lucille, who was Girlie to her friends. Girlie had all sorts of queer utensils in her place. Kathy would run down and ask her after a minute.

But first she hunted through the crumpled tissue for a card. These must be from Tommy, bless him. She remembered how once, in one of his more ardent and sentimental moments, Tommy had called her his wild Irish rose, born to blossom and unfold just for him....

And then she came on the envelope.

She drew out the card and her eyes widened as she read:

"Please accept the enclosure in the spirit in which it is sent. I am in your debt, my dear, not only because I was the unwitting cause of injustice to you, but because you have provided me with the first hearty laugh I have had in years. I refer to your little flare-up this morning. I have longed to say and do to a certain person precisely what you did. For years I have thought about it, but I am not a brave fellow and I lacked the courage. I do not wish any thanks for the enclosed check. Buy yourself some little knickknack with it that will make you happy. For myself I want nothing in return, unless perhaps you would grant a dull old fellow the privilege of dropping in to see you some day, to warm his hands at the glowing flame of your lovely youth. Your friend, Charley Whittaker."

So then Kathy picked up the envelope which she had tossed to the floor. And there inside was a check.

She opened it and looked at it and her eyes fairly popped out of her head. "Well, I'll be damned," she gasped.

It was a check for one thousand dollars.

CHAPTER SIX

Tommy laughed. Tommy said: "Well, baby, you certainly had me fooled. Here I had you figured as such a little innocent. And all the time you were being a smart girl—a very smart girl."

This was about an hour later. Tommy had come strolling in sooner than Kathy expected him. He seemed in quite a jolly mood. He was whistling, smiling, a charming young man without a care in the world. This was Tommy's invariable custom after they had quarreled. He rarely bothered to apologize or explain. It was much simpler, and certainly easier on the nervous system, simply to ignore the fact that there had been a row.

He had tossed his cap to a couch, and grabbed Kathy in his arms. "Hi, beautiful," he whispered, his tone husky, his long lazy blue eyes caressing her face. "Lord, baby, I'm nuts about you. Every time I take you in my arms, it's as exciting as it was the very first time. I'm always wondering to myself when the hell this feeling is going to wear off. With other women, it always wore off in a hurry. Once I had them, the thrill was gone. But with you it lingers on and on and on. Every time I walk into the room and see you, I can't wait to get you in my arms."

He kissed her passionately. "What is it about you, woman? Eh? What the hell is it?"

"I wouldn't know, Tommy."

Kathy relaxed in his embrace, giving herself up to the delight of his passionate eagerness for her. She closed her eyes. Her arms entwined themselves around his neck. The lovely, lovely blackness began to drift down around her. The blackness that was sifted with the brilliance of stars. The blackness that was a melting weakness and a fierce, primitive hunger for the love gratification from this man who appealed to her. The feeling that only Tommy could arouse in her.

He picked her up in his arms and carried her to a couch. And for a time Kathy lay with her eyes closed, reveling in the beautiful, beautiful sensations which only Tommy could arouse in her.

She thought, as her senses stirred with delight: This is a kind of heaven. This is all that really matters. I'd die if Tommy were to walk out on me. I'd simply die. What did it matter if Tommy spent his life talking about plays that he never wrote? What did it matter if he lived off her half the time? It's just his way, she told herself. If he were some other way, he wouldn't be Tommy. If he were the kind of man who would rather work in a boiler factory than borrow fifty cents from a girl then he wouldn't be Tommy. He wouldn't have Tommy's charm. He wouldn't have this devilish power to take her in his arms and arouse this torture of ecstasy in her.

He would be some entirely different person. And she wouldn't give a darn about him.

You can't have it both ways, she told herself wisely. If Tommy's what you want, then you'll have to take Tommy as he is. You'll have to put up with a Tommy who casually makes off with the rent money....

But when she thought of that, it occurred to her that she really should say something about it. No need of having another row about it. She didn't want any more rows with him. Not today. But he mustn't think he could get away with that and she not even mention it.

She pulled herself free of him, sat up, and asked Tommy for a cigarette. And when he had lit it for her she said, "By the way, honey, what became of that money I gave you to pay the bills with?"

Tommy was ready with a glib explanation, which he tossed off with an airy smile. "Oh, that's right," he said. "I meant to tell you about that."

It seemed there was a friend of Tommy's. Fellow he'd known for a long time. Old school chum, as a matter of fact. And a swell guy. A damn swell guy. But he was having a spot of rotten luck. Wife had had to go to the hospital suddenly. Serious operation. Very serious. Matter of life and death, really. And this guy without any money ahead. He'd been in the Army, and now he was out, and hadn't had the time to make a new connection.

Well, as luck would have it Tommy had run into him the very morning he was on his way over to the rental office with Kathy's money. "He asked me if I could loan him fifty bucks," Tommy said. "The poor guy was simply desperate. And I just didn't have the heart to turn him down. You wouldn't have wanted to turn down a guy in a fix like that, would you, honey?"

Kathy looked at him. She knew as well as she knew her name that Tommy was lying to her. She could feel it.

But if she told him so, she knew what would happen. Another ugly scene. And of course, there was always a chance that Tommy was telling the truth. It *could* be. "Don't you think you should have told me about it sooner?" she asked him.

Well, the guy had told him he could pay the money back in a day or so. "I figured he'd pay me back and then I could straighten everything out and you wouldn't need to know about it."

"I see," Kathy said. Her lips were set a little tight. She couldn't help that. It wasn't really Tommy's lying to her that she minded so much as she minded his taking her for a little sap who believed his lie. That she didn't like.

Tommy said shortly: "Don't you believe me?"

"Oh, sure, Tommy. Sure. I believe you."

"Well, you've got a funny look."

"Oh, you just imagine that."

"I'm not imagining anything. I can see what you're thinking. You can't fool me, baby. I know that look in your eye."

"Do you, Tommy?"

"Yes, I do. And by heck, I don't like it. You don't seem to have any faith in me, no matter what I do. I suppose you think I deliberately stole your dough. Maybe you think I spent it on some other dame. And if that's what you think, the hell with it. Is that what you think?"

"I said I believed you, Tommy."

"Yeah. You said it. With your tongue in your cheek. Why don't you believe me? Didn't you ever hear of a guy being out of dough, and having to send his wife to the hospital, and stuff like that? Don't you think a thing like that ever happens?"

"Oh, sure. I've heard of it happening. Lots of times. I guess it's one of the oldest stories in the world. By the way, Tommy, how is the wife? Is she getting along okay?"

"I don't know how the hell she is, and I don't give a damn. I'm sick of the whole mess. I'm sick of everything. I'm sick of the way you don't believe anything I tell you. Always ready to jump on me. Well, maybe I've got it coming. Maybe I deserve every bit of it."

Tommy jumped up and began to stride the floor. His eyes were moody; his shoulders dropped as if in utter dejection. "When you come right down to cases, why should you believe me? Why should you have any respect for me? I'm not much. I'm just a bum, that's what I am. No job, no dough. I let you feed me, give me a bed to sleep on. I'm no better than a kept man. Not a damn bit better. I try to kid myself. I tell myself I'm going to be a big-shot playwright. I've told myself over and over: Some day I'll repay every single thing

Kathy has done for me, and do a man sight more for her in return than she dreams of. That's what I tell myself. That's the only way I can look myself in the face. But maybe I'm all wet. Why don't I get wise to myself? Why the hell don't I? I don't amount to a damn. I'm just a penniless bum, that's what I am. Maybe it's all I ever will be. Oh, God, sometimes I wish I was dead. I wish I'd never been born. There's no peace for me, no peace anywhere. I'm burning up with ambition, but nothing comes of it. I'm just burning myself out. I love you like hell and all. But you think I'm playing you for a sucker. Some day you'll get tired of me and kick me out like a rat. Why don't you kick me out now, Kathy? Why don't you get it over with? I could crawl off in a gutter somewhere. Maybe I'd die there. And they'd collect me with the rest of the trash. Oh, God. I can't go on like this. I can't. I can't!"

And Tommy threw himself face down on the couch and began sobbing horribly.

Kathy stood, as she lit a fresh cigarette, and looked down at him. Her eyes, for a flickering moment, were astonishingly cool and clear. She thought: This is just one of his acts.

It wasn't the first scene of its kind. Whenever things were pressing too close for comfort, Tommy invariably contrived to stage a little act to play on her sympathy. Every time it had happened recently, one little side of Kathy's mind had seen it very clearly for what it was.

Tommy's way of getting around her.

Tommy's way of finishing, once and for all, an unpleasant argument that put him definitely in the wrong.

But for all of her shrewd, faintly bitter understanding of him, there was still the woman in her who loved him passionately and beyond all else.

And that woman flew to him, knelt beside him, put her hand gently to his cheek. "Don't go on like that, Tommy. Please. Get a grip on yourself. You're talking nonsense and you know it. Look, that's all right about the money. I was worried about it for a while. But it doesn't matter now. It doesn't matter a bit. The heck with that fifty bucks. Why, I almost forgot to tell you—I'm a rich woman!"

For a while she had completely forgotten Charley Whittaker's check. And there hadn't been a chance yet to tell Tommy about it.

Now she ran over to the table to find it.

"Do you believe in Santa Claus, Tommy?" she cried gaily. "Well, neither do I. Rather, I didn't. But lo and behold, he's paid me a visit. Look."

Tommy got a grip on himself and sat up. 'What the devil are you talking about?" he asked curiously.

"This," Kathy said, and she slipped down beside him and opened the check for him to see. "Look. It's real, Tommy. Anyway, I guess it is." She giggled. "Not that I'm any authority on checks for a thousand dollars."

"A thousand bucks!" Tommy stared at the thing, and then he stared at Kathy. "Say, what the hell's the idea? Do you mean to tell me that old coot sent you this? Why, my lassie? *Why?*"

So Kathy hurriedly told him the details. "I met him," she explained, "after I left you. Bumped into him right on Fifth Avenue. It was the funniest coincidence."

"Must have been," said Tommy unpleasantly. "I've heard of little coincidences like that before. So." He looked at her, and his eyes weren't nice. *"That's* why you were in such a rush to get away from me. That's why you picked a quarrel with me. I wondered about that after you walked off in such a rage. Because I hadn't said a darned thing for you to take offense at. Now I understand." He smiled. "Pretty neat work," he said. "Pretty neat."

Kathy stared at him. "Don't you believe me, Tommy?"

"Of course I don't believe you. What kind of a sap do you take me for?" He laughed again. "So you ran into him *quite* by accident. The *sheerest* coincidence. And that was—let's see—it was around noon when I met you. And it isn't five yet. Less than five hours ago. And already the old buzzard comes through with a thousand bucks. Fast work, Kathy old girl. Damned fast work. I didn't know you had it in you. It's the old story. The husband, or the boy friend, is always the last one to know. If you can make all that time in one little afternoon, you'll probably be moving into a penthouse in another week or so. You're moving right out of my class, baby. I can see that. Right out of my class. Well, it's been nice knowing you. And if the guy can afford it, you're worth the dough. You might tell him that for me. Or maybe he's already found that out for himself, the old skunk."

Kathy was too shocked and astonished to be angry. She just stared at Tommy. It had never occurred to her that he wouldn't believe her story. *She* knew it was true, so why shouldn't he believe it? He knew her so well. He knew she wouldn't lie to him. She said carelessly: "Oh, don't try to be funny, Tommy. You don't mean what you're saying. Why," she laughed, "only a few hours ago, you were telling me that I should make a play for some rich old guy. Now—"

"I did not tell you to make a play for him. I said, if you'd kid one of the old buzzards along a bit, you might get yourself some nice meals and drinks and maybe some little gifts that would— well, sort of make things easier for you. I figured some old guy like that would be glad to take a kid out to eat and dance and maybe give her some little gift, worth fifty bucks or so. And then you could trade it back for the dough and you wouldn't have to worry so about small change."

Kathy smiled. "You don't make much sense, Tommy. Rich guys don't usually hand out fifty-dollar gifts unless

they're getting something in return. And you know it as well
as the next one."

Which, of course, was just what she shouldn't have said.

"No?" said Tommy. "*No?*"

"No," said Kathy. "Anyway, that's the way I always heard it."
Her voice had an edge. She was beginning to get angry. "The fact
is, Tommy, when you were talking this morning, what you were
thinking was that maybe it would be a good idea for me to have a
little affair on the side with somebody. And I don't believe you'd
care. Because you think it would take my mind off your playing
around with Eunice Cairn and her ilk. People are always throwing it up to me, the way you trot after these middle-aged glamour
girls."

"Yeah?" said Tommy. "Oh, yeah? Well, you've certainly got
one heluva nerve, throwing anything up to me, the way you've
been pulling the wool over my eyes. I figured you were such a little innocent. And all the time you were being a smart girl, a very
smart girl. By the way, do you have a little private bank account
somewhere? How much more dough have you wangled out of
rich guys like old Whittaker?"

"I ought to slap your face for that," Kathy cried. And since
it was really a good idea, she did it. She slapped good and hard.
"You have a nerve saying a thing like that to me. I've told you and
told you how this happened. You can read his note. It's just an
innocent little gift because—well, because he felt he had lost me
my job and all. And I guess he really did get a kick out of the way
I told his wife off."

"Oh, sure he did. Sure. Guys like that just love having their
wives told off in public places by cheap little models. They love
having their wives kicked in the shins. They just love brawling
like that, and being made to look like silly asses. Well, I've often
heard of wealthy guys kicking through with plenty of cash to well

made little lovelies, but not for that reason. Never for *that* reason, my pet."

"You don't believe me, then," Kathy cried. "You don't believe a word I've been telling you."

"Nope." Tommy gave her a nasty smile. "I have your own words for it. How was it you said it? Rich guys don't hand out fifty-dollar gifts unless they're getting theirs in return. And I agree. So what do you expect me to think you've given old Money-Bags in return for a cool grand?"

Suddenly Tommy's eyes darkened. He moved toward her and his voice was thick. "But he's not going to have you all to himself, you little so-and-so." He had her in his arms, and she had never known such violence from him. His laugh came against her flesh, low, threatening, somehow evil. "He has to pay out big dough, but I can have you for free. He has to beg you, I'll bet. But I can make you beg me. Put your arms around me, you little wench. Hold me tight. Tighter. Tell me I'm the one you love. Tell me I'm the only one you really want. Go on. Tell me, damn you. Kiss me, you little devil. *Kiss me.*"

And then she knew his love, savage, angry, a little brutal. And as from a long way off she heard her own voice sobbing, furious, begging him to let her go; begging him not to spoil and destroy and make hideous every lovely thing that had been between them.

CHAPTER SEVEN

I T WAS around seven when Kathy went down to Lucille's apartment on the second floor. Lucille Moffat, who was Girlie to her pals, was fortyish and unworried about it. And sometimes when she became a little hilarious over too many drinks she would tell how she belonged to that bygone era when the gay young dogs used to call their sweeties "Girlie," and she would laugh and laugh about it. She had a stack of old love letters, and sometimes she would read a few of them aloud when she wanted to get a laugh. And no matter what man they were from, they would begin, "Dear girlie." Or "Dearest girlie." And sometimes, "My dearest, sweetest girlie." Anyway, she said they did.

Girlie had white hair which she wore in sleek, sculptured waves, a young face, and a thin, slightly caved in figure which, as she said, looked like nothing so much as a bag of bones when she was undressed. But when she put on clothes it was something else again. She could have walked down Fifth Avenue in a gunny sack, and somehow had so much dash that people would have turned to look at her. She had a greenish tweed suit which she'd worn for three winters and which had been spewed up by a bargain sale to start with. And she could still wear it, with tricky little hats and veils and a dash of costume jewelry, and look like a gal with a boy friend in the big chips.

And she was wise, too, was Girlie. Very wise. She was a woman who had long ago kissed her illusions goodbye. And she was Kathy's pal.

Kathy rushed in and found Girlie eating an onion sandwich, gooey with mayonnaise, and drinking beer. In between bites of the sandwich and sips of the beer, Girlie smoked a cigarette through a long ivory holder. She had on old slacks and a tight fitting yellow sweater, and she was so little and thin and vital-looking, if it hadn't been for her white hair you might have taken her for a kid of nineteen. Until you noticed her shrewd, wise eyes, of course. Kathy said, "Oh, Lord. You and your onion sandwiches."

Girlie smiled. "Thank heavens, I've reached the age when I can revel in onion sandwiches and not have to worry about keeping my breath glamorous for some man. Won't you have one, honey?"

Kathy shook her head. "No, thanks."

Girlie smiled, taking another big bite. She was seated on a couch with a bright red strip of velvet thrown over it. There was a little coffee table in front of the couch which she had painted an eye-shaking shade of blue. Girlie liked to surround herself with bright colors. On various tables around the room and on the high, old-fashioned mantel were small figurines which Girlie had modeled from clay. She had started out years before with the idea of becoming a famous sculptress. And she had almost made the grade. But not quite. She said now: "Tommy no likee onion breath, eh? Well, some day you'll get across the Bridge of Sighs, honey." By which Girlie meant the period of sighing and weeping over men. It was one of her expressions.

"Then you'll learn that men who make passes are fun, but eating what you darn please is more fun. By the way, how is Tommy?"

Kathy's dark eyes flashed. She drew up an ottoman and sank down on it. "The hell with that heel," she said. "I've just told him to get out. I gave him an hour to pack his stuff and scram. I came down here while he did it. I told him I never wanted to lay eyes on him again. And I don't, either. I hate that guy."

"Like that, eh?" Girlie arched a hair-line brow. Her cool gray eyes were thoughtful. "Want to tell me what happened?"

So Kathy told her. "He believes I let old Charley Whittaker make time with me. He actually *believes that.*"

"And didn't you?" Girlie asked pleasantly.

Kathy groaned. "You too!"

"Now look, honey. I just want to get the set-up straight. It is rather a fantastic story, you know. I've lived a long time, and most of it around New York, but I've never seen any rich guys handing out fancy checks with no strings attached. I suppose it could happen. The man might have softening of the brain or something of that sort. But I just never happened to hear of it happening."

"You're just like Tommy," Kathy said indignantly. "You don't have any faith in people."

"Not a bit," Girlie said cheerfully. "By the way, this old boy didn't offer to buy you the Empire State building? Nothing like that?"

"You seem to think he's nuts?"

"He doesn't sound like a man who was quite himself." And Girlie laughed. She got up and went over to a little ice chest which was draped with a piece of oriental tapestry. She came back with a couple of more bottles of beer. She filled a tall, thick amber-colored glass and handed it to Kathy. "Go to work on this, honey, and you'll feel more cheerful. I wouldn't get too much of a hate on Tommy. After all, he's just a man. Men are very crude people, honey. They're only one jump out of the cave and they regard all other men as wolves. And after all, they're right."

"You're taking Tommy's part," Kathy said moodily, sipping at the beer. "If you could have seen how he treated me. I thought he was going to tear my hair out. I honestly did. And I won't stand for that sort of thing, and for being called a lying little tramp besides. Look. Look here, Girlie."

Kathy had slipped into a green corduroy housecoat, and now she slipped the sleeve of it up. "Look at this bruise on my arm. *That's* what he did to me, the brute."

Girlie laughed brightly. "You and Babs ought to get together and compare your bruises. You might hold a competition. I'll tell you what, honey. You throw a party tonight, and we'll all toddle up and vote on the prowess of your men, Fred and Tommy. And I'll present the prize. I have just the very thing. It will make a lovely prize. Come here and I'll show you."

Girlie got up and sauntered down the room to a long table at the far end which was her work table. For years now, Girlie had made her living decorating little pottery novelties. She had a little basement shop in the Village, a block or so away, where she sold her things. She still worked at her sculpturing in odd hours, but this was more of a hobby. She made very little at it. Her decorated pottery articles, ash trays, flower vases, decorative dolls, all manner of odds and ends; paid her rent and food bills.

Now, on the long table, was a most extraordinary collection of articles. Kathy stared, and she began to giggle. "Why, Girlie, what on *earth*—" She picked up one by the small handle and giggled some more. Not since she was a kid had she seen one of these, and then under her grandmother's bed, with a crocheted cover over the lid of it. Girlie smiled "We'll call it a utensil *de chambre*, to be coy about it."

There were a dozen or more of them, all practically alike. And Girlie had been glamorizing them by painting Cupids around the sides. "Or we might call it a modern soup tureen," Girlie added.

"Soup tureen!" Kathy stared.

"That's what people are buying them for, believe it or not. I picked these up in an old Fifth Avenue house. They'd been up in the attic for years. I paid ten cents apiece, and after I fix them up I sell them for five bucks."

"You mean people actually *buy* them? Pay real money for them?"

"They sell like hot cakes. If I could get enough, I could make a small fortune on them. They've become the rage. Honest. A dealer was in the other day and offered me two dollars apiece if I could find some *small* ones. He thought they'd make fine beer mugs. But these large ones are wonderful for soup. Anyway, so the society women tell me."

Kathy shook her head. "Well, I've sometimes wondered what this world was coming to."

"And there you have it, honey. The pot has come out from under the bed and gone onto the table for soup. Isn't it sweet? But anyway, as I was suggesting—about your party tonight—you and Babs compare your bruises. And the winner gets one of these. How's that for an idea?"

Kathy laughed. And then she looked doleful. "But there won't be any party. A lot I feel like making whoopee, with Tommy and me split up." She hated to admit it, even to herself, but already she was weakening about Tommy; beginning to wonder if she had been too hasty.

She walked slowly back to the ottoman and picked up her beer glass. She finished the beer that was in it, and Girlie insisted on pouring some more. "Beer relaxes you," Girlie said. "You need to relax. You're like a violin that's strung too tight. You aren't seeing things straight. You don't want to split up with Tommy, honey. Not over this Whittaker business. You'll only let yourself in for a lot of grief you know."

"But you've never liked Tommy. You've told me over and over I was wasting my time."

"Yes. Of course. So I have. And so you are. But a child wastes a lot of time having measles, and other children's diseases. You waste time you could be at school or at play. But there's nothing to be done about it until the fever burns itself out. With you Tommy Terry is a disease. A disease that hasn't burned itself out. He's still in your blood. If you let him go while it's like that, you'll never be really free of him. You won't be free to love some other man."

"I tell you I hate Tommy. I hated him today." She got up and wandered aimlessly around the room.

"Sure. I know. That's just the trouble. As long as you're so steamed up over a man you'll go to the bother of hating him, it's a sure sign you're still that way over him."

"You think a woman can love a man and hate him both at the same time?"

"Certainly. Why not? Not that I've ever believed you really love Tommy. I don't believe you know what love is."

Kathy laughed shortly. "Don't be silly, Girlie. I've been out of my mind about that guy. No one knows better than little Kathy what a sucker I've been. I've fed him. I've bought his clothes for him. I've loaned him money that I could certainly have used for myself. I waste my time kidding him along about his writing, when I certainly have my doubts as to whether he'll ever write a line worth writing. And I put up with his running after those middle-aged tootsies, because one of them may come through and back one of his plays, *he sez*. And if all that isn't love, what is it?"

"Just a curious form of insanity," Girlie said pleasantly. "And now I think you'd better scram. Make it up with Tommy—"

"He'll be gone by now," Kathy said gloomily.

"Oh, no, he won't. If I know that charming young dead-beat of yours, he hasn't the faintest idea of going. Where would he go to? You'll probably find him right where you left him, getting drunk, no doubt, to drown his sorrow. On your liquor, of course."

"I told him to go and he'll be gone."

"Oh, don't be silly," Girlie snapped impatiently. "Won't you ever learn anything about men? He'll be there, waiting to ask you to forgive him. And you hurry up and forgive him. It's always simpler to forgive them and get it over with. Save such a lot of talk and energy. And you have the party to get ready for. Oh, by the way, now that you're flourishing big checks around, how's about making it a little champagne spree? I haven't tasted champagne in ages. And I did so used to love it, when I still had what it took to wangle it out of the gents. Phone Jerry. He usually has champagne on hand. Tell him to put it on my bill, and you can pay me after you cash that check which I still don't believe you got for being an honest woman. If you did, you're a smarter gal than I ever was. I'll round up the kiddies and we'll make this a real night."

Which reminded Kathy unpleasantly of Henry Peterson. She sent Girlie a wry grin as she went toward the door. "I've been warned against having a noisy party tonight. Seems as if it might bring on a miscarriage."

Girlie looked startled.

"Why, *honey!* You didn't tell me there was anything like that. When? Who? *Tommy?*"

"Oh, not me." Kathy giggled. "Anyway, I hope not. Hattie Peterson. There's due to be a little Peterson almost any time now."

"Oh, her. I don't believe it. I think it's all her imagination. She's a little batty, in case you didn't know."

"I thought *he* was."

"Both of them. It's my private opinion they were both dropped on their heads when they were babies, and never got over it. Anyway, this is a free country, isn't it? At least, it's supposed to be. It's still free enough so that the wacky Petersons can't prevent our having a little fun. If he makes any objections," Girlie laughed, "I know what we'll do. We'll hurl one of my soup tureens at his head. And I'll wager *that* will quiet him down."

"And maybe out," Kathy grinned. But she agreed it was a pretty idea.

CHAPTER EIGHT

G IRLIE knows my Tommy better than I do, Kathy thought ruefully, when she opened her door. Because there he was, just as Girlie had said he would be, stretched out on one of the couches, with a half empty bottle of Kathy's precious gin on the floor beside him. He moved a little, lifting his head, when he heard her walk across the room. He held out his hand to her. "Don't send me away, kid," he begged. He seemed the picture of utter dejection. "If you kick me out, I'm sunk. You're the only beautiful thing I have to hold to in this rotten, lousy world. Nobody but you gives a damn about me. Let me stay, honey. I was a heel to you. I'll go on my knees and grovel to you. I'm not fit to kiss the ground you walk on. Come here, honey. Put your arms around me. Tell me you'll forgive me. I lost my head completely. But it was only because I'm so damned nuts about you. Why do we keep fighting, sweetheart? We oughtn't to fight when we love each other so much. Come here, baby. Kiss me. *Kiss me.*"

So Kathy kissed him and forgave him and then she told him about the party. "You run over to Jerry's, honey. Girlie wants champagne." Which seemed to annoy Tommy. He sat up, pushing back his hair which could have stood a little cutting. But Tommy liked it long. He felt that it made him look artistic.

"So *Girlie* wants champagne," he said. "Who's giving this party? You or her? Why does that witch always have to run everything?"

Kathy was dashing about the room, straightening things a little. Charley's American Beauty roses were on a wooden orange crate which masqueraded as a table. Kathy had put them in the garbage pail, and wound it with green tissue paper. She considered the result quite effective. "Now don't start griping about Girlie," she said.

"That dame don't like me," Tommy scowled. He picked up the gin bottle and took a long swallow. "She's against me."

"Oh, Tommy, for heaven's sake. You always think people are against you. Girlie's your friend. Why, she's the one who insisted that I come back and make up with you. She thought it was perfectly silly for us to quarrel just because—"

"Oh. So you've been talking me over with her. *She* said to make up with me. I suppose you run to her with everything that happens between us. *She* has to know all our private affairs. I guess, if I knew the truth, *she's* been encouraging you to have an affair with some old goat like Whittaker."

Kathy stopped smack in the middle of the room and gave him a look. "Now look, Tommy, I'm warning you. Don't start that again. If you have any sense at all, you'll skip the whole subject. And you'll skip *this* for the present, too." And she walked over and took the gin bottle away from him.

"Now shake a leg and get on over to Jerry's. You'll have to get some stuff to eat, too. Here's my book of points. You'll need that for the cheese. I don't suppose cheese and rye bread are precisely the thing to go with champagne. Or are they? Anyway, I can't think of anything else. Get anything you see that looks good. And you'd better buy a dozen candles. Since thanks to you, you louse, there isn't any electric light."

She had already lit two tall candles, one at either end of a big old trunk which she had draped with cretonne and used to stack books. She always kept a few candles on hand. She liked to lie there in the dim flickering light and have Tommy make love to her.

Finally she got him off. She scurried into the little kitchen compartment to wash her collection of old jelly glasses which would serve for the champagne. All of her plates and saucers were cracked or chipped, and not one of them matched another in design. But none of her guests would think anything of that. Although they would have been more or less horrified had she produced a set of dishes which were intact.

It was getting chilly, so she got the coal which she kept in an old-fashioned bucket beside the kitchen gas range. She crumpled some old newspapers, stuck them in the little round belly of the stove, set them to blazing and dumped the coal on top of the flames. The bright blaze would die down in a couple of minutes and then the coal would burn along lazily for two or three hours.

These practical matters attended to, Kathy ran behind the curtain of her improvised dressing room to put on fresh makeup and redo her hair. She thought of a quick bath, but that meant running down to the third floor. And no doubt someone else would be using the bathroom when she got there. Too much bother.

She lit another candle on her little dressing table. Darn Tommy. This not having any real light was getting her down. Candles were all right for atmosphere. But when you wanted to make up your face, you wanted to *see*. However, she made out.

She painted herself a lovely, wide bright mouth and brushed and brushed at her dark curls until they were a cloud of dancing waves framing her small, vivid face. For the street she liked to part her hair in the middle and smooth it back sleekly to a small knot. She thought that style gave her quite an air.

But for a party, she liked it loose and flowing.

She still wore her black gym trunks under the housecoat and she decided not to take them off. A spot of dancing might be indicated before the party was over, and the little satin tights would come in handy. She took off the housecoat and slipped on black satin lounging pajamas and a loose, flame-colored jacket with a design of glittering green and red and blue stones over each breast. She shook back her curls and looked in the mirror. Her eyes were bright and glowing and enormous. The jacket brought her alive with color. She looked cute. She looked cute as hell.

Which was what Fred said when he arrived with Babs, who had forgiven him his mistreatment of her and was in a lovey-dovey mood. Fred was a tall, dark, rather good-looking man and really not a bad fellow in many ways—when he was sober. Only he was practically never sober. He came in and put his arms around Kathy and kissed her on the mouth. "Holy Moses, you look cute, honey," he said. And he kissed her a second time, more seriously.

It was the second kiss which seemed to annoy Babs. "Look, you big hunk of flesh on the hoof," she said. "I don't mind your *kissing* Kath, but kindly let it stop right there. Don't forget you're married to me, sonny boy."

"Am I?" Fred gave her a funny grin, and then he slipped his arm around her. "Well, look, I'm the kind of a guy who could use two wives. How's about us trotting off someplace where a man can have as many wives as he wants? That system always appealed to me. Hell, nature never intended for a big, husky man to confine himself to one dame all his life. It ain't natural. Say, Kathy my pet, did you ever hear the story about the old guy who took his wife out to look at a prize bull? And the guy said to the keeper of the bull—"

"No." Kathy grinned. "And I don't want to hear it. Look, Tommy's due with some champagne any minute. Until he arrives, all I can produce is gin." Fred trottled after her as she went to get the gin bottle.

He kept trying to put his arms around her, and Babs didn't like it. Her face began to freeze up, as she walked over to the table and lit a cigarette. Kathy didn't want Babs to go into one of her "states." It would ruin the party before it ever began. But she couldn't keep Fred away from herself.

Fred seemed fascinated by a certain little curl behind Kathy's right ear. He kept reaching for it, playing with it. Kathy said, under her breath: *"Please*, Fred—" And Fred said: "About this question of me taking a couple of wives, the idea fascinates me. Maybe that's what's wrong with my life. I never had enough wives."

"You lecher, you," Babs screamed suddenly. "You keep away from Kath. You let her alone. You stop mooching around her, or I—I—"

Kathy hurried to pour the gin and pass it around. Anything to quiet Babs down. "Don't pay any attention to Fred, darling. You know he doesn't mean anything."

"I want another wife," Fred insisted, after he'd tossed the gin down, straight, without so much as batting an eye.

Kathy took her own gin, and for some reason it went promptly to her head. Perhaps because she hadn't had any dinner. Or lunch either, she remembered suddenly. She'd completely forgot about eating.

She began to giggle. "Sure, I'll be your second wife," she kidded Fred. She took another sip of the gin. "I'll be anybody's wife who believes that I'm an honest woman. We won't count Tommy, of course."

"Why won't you count Tommy? Why the hell don't I count?" That was Tommy stumbling in, laden down with packages and bottles. You could tell right off that Tommy had taken time while he was out for a couple of quick ones. His eyes were bloodshot and his voice was a little thick.

Fred tossed off another shot of gin. "My fren," he said, advancing toward Tommy, "I'm considering taking Kathy for my second wife." He shook a finger in Tommy's face. "We're buddies, aren't we, chum? We might have been cut off the same pattern. We might have been Siamese twins, by heck. We both were born to be great writers, weren't we? Tell me that, chum, weren't we?"

"Sure," said Tommy.

"The spark of genius burns within us. Right?"

"Right."

"But do we write? I'm asking you, pal. Do we? No. I'll tell you the answer. We don't. We're no damn good, either one of us. We're just two rotten, drunken, lousy bums. Right?"

"Right," said Tommy, grinning. He was tugging at the cork of one of the champagne bottles, which suddenly gave with an explosive pop.

"Right. Shake on it, brother." And Fred held out his hand and insisted on shaking hands earnestly. "We agree. We're just a couple of bums. We let these two nice, sweet, beautiful, wonderful girls go out and work for us while we lie around and sip at the well-known grape that deadens initiative. We let the spark of genius within us die, while the gals bring home the bread and gin. Right?"

Babs said: "Oh, my Lord. I thought I had him sobered up, and already he's as high as a kite. Fred, for heaven's sake, shut up. It isn't ten o'clock yet. Do you have to start making a complete ass of yourself before ten o'clock?"

Fred turned to her gravely. "Woman, keep a civil tongue in your head."

Kathy said: "I want some food. I feel that gin. It's because I haven't had anything to eat all day. Honey," to Tommy, "give me a piece of bread and a hunk of cheese. The rest of you can feed your own pusses. Don't expect me to wait on you. Some cheese, my love. I'm perishing for cheese."

Tommy cut some bread and handed it to her with a thick slice of Swiss cheese, and Kathy sank down on the floor on a cushion and began nibbling greedily. "Gosh, that tastes good." She sipped some champagne, lit a cigarette.

But Fred was still right on Tommy's coat-tail. "You haven't answered me, my friend," he insisted, taking a moment off to see if he could safely balance the champagne glass on the tip of his nose. He couldn't. The glass smashed to the floor and the liquor began to dribble out. Fred picked it up. "Heluva thing," he said. "I must be getting old. Can't do a simple little trick like that. It's all a matter of coordination. When a man can't coordinate, he's finished. Now see here, my friend, as I was saying, isn't it true that neither of us is any damn good? We're just a couple of lazy, booze-fighting bums, aren't we? We call ourselves Village artists. But we're really bums. Right?"

"Oh, sure. You're right. Why don't you go over there in the corner and sleep it off?"

"Well, here's what I'm getting at. We share all these other things in common, so why shouldn't we share our wives in common?"

"But I'm not Tommy's wife." Kathy's voice came, giggly with champagne. It had tasted so good, and she had taken too much in a hurry. "I'm just the girl friend, never a wife. Tommy doesn't want to marry me, do you, darling? Tommy thinks I belong to the kept sisterhood." She giggled again. "Tommy thinks I've snatched a naughty, rich old banker. Don't you think that, my pet?"

It was the champagne talking, of course. And Tommy glowered at her. "You'd better stick to the cheese and pass up the champagne," Tommy warned her.

"But I like champagne," Kathy insisted. "It makes me feel good and warm and bubbly inside. It makes me love everybody. Maybe if I drink enough I could go for my banker—"

"What's all this about a banker?" That was Jack Dalby, who drew charcoal nudes. And very good ones, too, although the Post Office Department might not have approved of them going through the mails. He came strolling into the room, a tall, thin, anaemic-looking man with restless hands and a mincing walk. He talked in a shrill, worried voice.

And then a couple of others arrived. A dark, intense girl named Muriel whose sensitive, beautiful, immortal (she thought) poems never sold. And who, it was rumored, was taking to doped cigarettes to help her forget that she had been forced to sell her soul by writing cheap, sentimental love stories which did find a market. But she could never bring herself to write one of the sickly, revolting things until she was on the verge of starvation.

Muriel was flourishing a check, and her eyes were bitter. "Look at this damned thing," she cried. "I bare the recesses of my soul, and I get a check for thirty-three miserable bucks."

Someone cried: "You should have Kathy teach you the art of making bankers and winning checks. She has a check for a thousand bucks, and according to her she didn't bare anything. If you can believe that. Does anyone here believe it?" That was Babs, who was sore at Kathy because of Fred's interest in her.

Girlie arrived at that point, creating a moment's diversion with one of her "soup tureens."

The crowd howled and Girlie grinned. "Now, now, chillen. No funny cracks. We're supposed to be a group of artists. So let's not.be too obvious in our wisecracks. This is *my* latest artistic creation. I'm just like Muriel, only different. Twenty years different I sell my soul for any kind of money that comes along. And I love it."

Muriel groaned. "There's no chance for an artist. We're ground down. We're *crucified.*" She found herself a glass of champagne and went over to a corner and, for no particular reason, began to sob.

"Kathy has you all beat." That was Babs again, making a jealous jibe. "Kathy is going in for big money. Why don't we all sit at Kathy's feet and learn the ways of life?"

"What's Kathy done?" That was a sweet young thing who had just arrived in the Village, and hadn't decided if she'd rather be a great actress, a writer of sonnets, or just an old-fashioned wife—if she could find herself an attractive man.

"Kathy has found herself a banker."

"Oh, goodie. However did you do it, Kathy? I'd love to find me a banker. Has he any sex appeal? Wouldn't a rich banker with lots of sex appeal be just too, too heavenly!"

It went on like that. And on. And on. Kathy kept drinking more than she should, and talking more than she had ever intended to. She told over and over how she had kicked Charley Whittaker's wife in the shins, and he had sent her a check for a thousand dollars.

But no one would believe that she had kept her honor intact.

Tommy didn't believe her, the skunk.

Girlie didn't believe her. And Girlie was her pal.

Babs didn't believe her.

No one believed her. No one at all. She had never intended to mention a word about it. But it all came spilling out.

She saw Tommy glowering at her. Tommy was getting high. And the more he drank, the more he glowered. He was furious at her for talking about it. Well, why shouldn't she talk about it? It was a good story. And it was her story. It had actually happened to her.

Fred kept drinking, and would always come back to his original point. Now why shouldn't he take two wives? "Sure, honey," he said to Kathy. "Sure I'll marry you, even if you did make a little time with the banker. The more bankers, the better. That's just the kind of a wife I'm looking for—a gal who has a couple bankers on the side. Then I'd never have to worry again over the meal problem. I wish Babs was as practical as you are. Now Babs here, she never looks at any man but me. And where is that going to get the two of us?"

"Do you want me to go and get another man?" Babs cried furiously and drunkenly. "Do you? Oh, dear heaven, how can I bear it? You live off me, you beat me up. Oh, don't try to pshh me. Everybody knows how you mistreat me. And now you want me to get another lover."

Things were getting a little too intense, and Kathy had the bright idea that a little dancing might prove a convenient diversion. The emotional tension was getting a little too stark. Next thing, somebody would start a fight. She darted up and stepped out of the black pajamas. Tossed off her flame jacket.

And there she was, a darting little flash of fire, her curls flying, eyes too bright, the trunks no more than a ribbon of silk around her slender, beautiful legs. She cried gaily: "I can't marry you, Fred, because Babs wouldn't like it. Babs would cut my throat, wouldn't you, darling? And anyway, you don't believe I'm an honest woman either. You want me—plus the banker. I'm holding out for a man who believes my story. I won't marry any man who doesn't believe me, even if he thinks I'm lying. So until a guy like that turns up, I think I'll dance."

"Nobody asked you to dance," Babs snapped. "You're always wanting to show yourself off. You seem to think you're the only dame in the world with legs. My God, haven't we *all* got legs?"

"Not like Kathy's," Fred put in maliciously, which sent Babs into a fresh fury.

She asked everyone in the room, her eyes on each in turn as they lounged, most of them on the floor, propped against cushions: "Why do I put up with him? Why don't I kill him?"

Kathy began to do a tap dance. Her legs flashed, her curls flew, her feet clicked. She really was good at it. She was just getting really into her stride when a mild voice from the doorway said: "May I come in?"

Everyone turned to look. Kathy stopped dead to look. And then she gasped: "Oh, for goodness sakes." It was Charley Whittaker.

There was nothing for Kathy to do but go over and invite him in. "I happened to be out late at a banquet," Charley Whittaker said in his quiet pleasant way, "and I was walking home. I always enjoy walking at night. It refreshes me somehow. Well, I was passing near here. And I happened to remember you lived in this neighborhood. So I took the liberty of dropping in. Do you mind?"

"Of course not," Kathy said brightly. She was thankful now she'd had all that champagne. She could never have managed to handle this situation gracefully without a little liquor to fortify her. "Come right in, Mr. Whittaker. I want you to meet my friends." And she introduced him around.

Mr. Whittaker smiled in his pleased, almost naïve way. "Well," he said, "this is certainly nice. This is quite an experience for me. I've so often wished I could join a Greenwich Village group." He laughed a trifle. "I suppose none of you would believe it, but I've a touch of the Bohemian in me. Buried rather deep, of course."

Kathy was helping him off with his coat. She brought him champagne. Girlie made a place for him on the floor beside her, and patted a cushion invitingly. "You'd better come over beside me, Charley. I'm practically a Gay Nineties model myself."

Charley took a sip of his champagne. "Well, now," he said, "you're all very gracious to me, I'm sure. I won't be intruding?" he inquired doubtfully. "I won't spoil the party if I stay a while?"

"Of course not," Kathy said.

Jack Dalby spoke up in his high-pitched voice. "Perhaps you could persuade Kathy to pose in the nude, old scout. I've been wanting to do a charcoal nude of her. But the silly child won't part with those nasty old clothes. She seems to imagine clothes are important, for some reason."

Charley considered this suggestion thoughtfully. His eyes went to Kathy. Kathy flushed, her eyes bright. Charley smiled. "Well, now, I'm sure Miss Kathy would make a very lovely subject for an artistic drawing. But then, she's very lovely as she is. Very lovely."

Something like a muttered curse came from Tommy's lips and Girlie spoke up hurriedly. "Better come over here, Charley, right beside of me. Kathy was doing a tap dance. I'm sure you'll enjoy watching that."

But instead of going directly over to Girlie, Charley thought that he'd like another little sip of champagne. Not *too* much, just a little. So they all had another round. And then Fred, who had left the room for a moment, returned with the makings of whiskey highballs. By the time that was over and they'd each had a stiff highball or two, there wasn't a sober breath left in the room.

Certainly Charley wasn't sober. He had become unbelievably arch and gay. And it occurred to him that he, too, would like to do a tap dance. "You wouldn't believe it," Charley said, "but I was quite a one for tapping when I was a youngster. Yes-siree. I was quite a tapper."

"Let's see you do it, Charley. Come on. Swing a leg. Get hot. Let's see you do your stuff."

Hands began to clap, Kathy began to tap, and Charley ripped off his coat and collar and began to tap right along with her.

He wasn't bad. He was remarkably light on his feet for an old fellow whose days and years had been spent dutifully and dully in the realms of high finance. He stopped once for another drink, and laughed gaily. "Not bad, am I, for an old fellow? What do you think, Kathy?" And he caught Kathy and gave her a quick kiss. "Didn't I tell you I wasn't as old as you thought I was? Didn't I tell you?"

Kathy felt Tommy watching her. She caught Babs looking at her. Fred said something which Tommy didn't like, and she saw Tommy's fist shoot out. Now they were going to fight, and that might develop into anything. She must stop it somehow. Get their minds off it. She caught Charley's hand. "Come on, old sport. Back into your stuff."

They began to tap again, and the sweet young thing giggled and decided to join them. And the next thing, practically everyone in the room had joined in. Everyone except Fred and Tommy, who were over at one end of the room, still muttering at each other. The noise by this time was enough to jar the dead. Dishes rattled, the floor shook. It sounded like bedlam. Kathy, out of one corner of her eye, saw Tommy's fist shoot out again. A left to Fred's jaw. And then she saw Fred come back at him. She yelled something to them. "Look, you guys—" Charley Whittaker was going like a whirling dervish. "Isn't this fun?" he cried. "I declare, I don't know when I've had such fun."

Girlie yelled back at him: "Enjoy yourself, chum. You only live once."

And then a flustered, angry little man came bustling into the room, his cheeks quivering, his fists going. It was Henry Peterson.

"I warned you," he squeaked. "I *warned* you. And you wouldn't listen. I have had to call the ambulance for my wife. Now I shall call the police. I shall put a stop to this carrying on, or know the reason why."

As one man, they all ganged up to give him the bum's rush. "You old joy-killer," someone cried. "You can't have any fun yourself, so you don't want anyone else to have any."

Kathy was giggling hysterically. "It's that silly Henry Peterson," she cried, pointing a finger at him. "Isn't he silly-looking? Isn't he?" And then she added for no reason: "Why don't you go get a haircut? A man who's going to have a baby should certainly blow himself to a haircut."

They were slowly moving up on him, forcing Mr. Peterson to back his way angrily out of the room. "I warned you," he kept saying. "You can't say I didn't warn you."

And then, somehow, Girlie moved to the head of the procession, her soup tureen in hand. "Get going, smart guy," she said calmly. "And don't come back." And as Henry went galloping down the stairs, she aimed, and through sheer magic sent the tureen spinning to land square on top of his head.

Then they stood there at the top of the stairs in the narrow hallway, laughing at Henry's discomfiture. "Isn't it a scream? Isn't it beautiful? How did you ever do it, Girlie? Look! He can hardly get it off. Oh, goodie, goodie, there it comes. Well, that'll learn you, smart guy. Try to spoil a little innocent fun, will you? Oh, dear, did you ever, ever see anything so funny!"

Charley Whittaker seemed a trifle worried. "Do you suppose he could be seriously hurt?"

"Oh, heavens, no. A little solid earthenware couldn't crack *that* thick skull. There's nothing in it, anyway. Just a lot of screws rattling."

"But do you think he was in earnest about calling the police?" This seemed to remind Charley Whittaker that perhaps he'd better be going. He made a quick dash for his hat and coat and was on his way, when another figure came leaping up the steps, two at a time.

Kathy recognized Matt Dexter. She stood there in the hall, scowling at him. "Well," she said, "I might have known you'd show up. I suppose you can't stand a little noise either, and you're here to throw me out."

"You certainly made a hell of a racket," Matt said, and he wasn't smiling. "And you've spoiled a whole evening's work for me. But we'll skip that. You'd better get rid of your little pals, and quick. That guy has already called the police. They're probably on their way here now."

Kathy began to look worried. "But we weren't doing anything. Only having a little fun." She was still a little tight, so she added, giggling: "Something happened to me today, only no one would believe it happened the way I said it did. That's really how all the commotion started."

"Sure," Matt said. "Parties always start somehow. Anything can start one. And the next thing you know, some guy is laid out cold."

"But no one in here is out cold, Matt Dexter. What are you talking about? We're all good pals in here. It was only that no one would believe my story, and that made me sore. So I offered to marry anyone who did believe me. That's what I'm looking for, Matt. There must be one man somewhere who will believe that I'm an honest woman. Do you believe me?"

"Sure. I'd believe anything you told me. That's the kind of a guy I am—a great sucker for any story, if the girl is cute enough."

"Well, that's certainly big of you, Matt. Maybe you'd like to marry me," Kathy suggested sweetly. "Would you? Because I said I would. I said any man who believed me—"

"Nope," said Matt. "I wouldn't care to marry you."

"Why not?"

"You aren't my type."

"But, listen—"

"You listen, you little dope." And he brushed past her and on into the room. "I don't want to marry you, and I don't think you have any sense. But you're cute, and I sort of like you even though you are a dope, and I'd like to help you out of a tough spot. Don't you even know you're in a spot? Are you too high to realize what's going on here? Well, have a look."

So Kathy looked, and her eyes bulged. There was Tommy on the floor, dead to the world. And Fred was leaning over him and so was Babs. Fred was muttering: "But he socked me first. You all saw him go at me. He was jealous because of something I said to Kathy. And I didn't mean to hit him that hard."

Matt took charge. He leaned over Tommy for a moment, felt his pulse. "He'll come out of it," he said shortly. "But get him out of here. All of you get out. If you don't you're going to have a nice spot of explaining to do to the police. Now all of you bums, move. Get going. And take this lug with you," meaning Tommy.

So they moved, and fast.

They weren't exactly scared of the police. After all, what had they done? But Tommy *was* out cold. And heaven only knew what kind of a story that wacky Henry Peterson might tell. It was getting late anyway. It was high time to be going....

One by one they disappeared.

All in a moment, it seemed, the room was emptied out. It was as quiet as a church. There was only the litter of glasses and dishes and cushions around the floor. The fire in the little pot-bellied stove had died out. And so had the candles. Only two dim candles were still burning. The wax melted and slowly hardened. Over in the far corner, the bright roses were beginning to droop.

There were only these things, and Kathy and Matt Dexter.

She stood there looking up at him in the dying flicker of light. He was so tall. She hadn't realized how tall he was. And his eyes looked so dark and his teeth so white as he smiled down at her. An odd, unknown excitement stirred in her as she stood there looking up at him.

She gave a little ghost of a laugh. "Well," she said, "now that you've broken up the party, aren't you going too?"

"No," said Matt. "I think I'll stick around awhile."

CHAPTER NINE

M ATT DEXTER said: "You're certainly fun to love, beautiful."

"Am I?"

"Um-hum."

"How nice?"

"Awfully nice. You have the prettiest black hair—"

"Do you like black hair, Matt?"

"I like your hair. And I like your nice, smooth skin and your great big eyes. And when it comes to a cute little figure—You've got everything, gorgeous. Everything a man wants, for one little night of love.... "

This was later. Much later. Matt had, as he had said, decided to stick around for a little while. He hadn't intended to stay too long. He didn't want to get mixed up with any little Village tootsie. Heck, he didn't want to get mixed up with any woman. Not yet. Not for a long time. But he had gone without a woman for months and months. Gone without so much as a few gay parties with women along.

There had been all that stretch of time when he was out in the far Pacific, nearly two years of it. When he had learned all about the hell of war. About the stench and the bombs and the filth and the loneliness and the awful, awful screams of the dying. He had come home at last, with three citations for bravery. One for saving a trapped comrade from almost certain death.

He had come home with two Jap bullets in his chest, and after that there had been the long siege in the hospital when pneumonia had developed, and for a time the doctors hadn't given him one chance in a hundred to pull through.

It was during the long, endless days of his convalescence that Matt had had plenty of time to go into the woman question with himself, and decide just where he stood.

His decision was that he was through with them for many a long day to come.

He wasn't exactly bitter about that girl—Jenny her name was—who had melted in his arms with extravagant promises of undying devotion *before* he went off to war, and then, in time, sent him the inevitable letter. She would always remember him—as a dear, good, kind friend. But she was going to marry another man.

Nope, he wasn't bitter about it. And he didn't hold anything against Jenny. It wasn't her fault that he had allowed all his youthful dreams and emotions to center upon her, any more than it was her fault that another man had come along who looked like a better bet.

Heck, he wasn't any bargain in any woman's language.

Not when he was chained to a bed in a service hospital, with maybe one lung gone, no money to speak of, and nothing certain about the future except his hopes and his ambitions, and a certain gift for objective writing which had already put a couple of his war stories into one or two leading magazines.

She'd have been a damn fool if she had stuck with me, Matt would tell himself.

But just the same he had loved Jenny like hell and all.

She was the only girl he had ever loved or ever told that he loved. And when she walked out of his life, it seemed to him that she took all the years of his youth with her. And his dreams and his faith in a kind of love for which there were no words, but to which a man holds when he is young, and before experience has taught him that love, after all, is only another name for sexual desire. And that women are all more or less alike.

You could group all women, he told himself now, into two classes: the ones you wanted to make, and the ones you didn't. Well, from now on he would take his fun with the ones who appealed to him, when there were not more important matters to engage his energies.

But the heck with allowing himself a special feeling for any one of them. Some day, when he got around to it, when he had made his way, when he was in the chips and could afford it, he would pick himself some nice, well educated girl with enough looks to get by and a good sense of humor, and he'd marry her and settle down.

But all that was a long time in the future. For the time being he didn't want to get mixed up with any of them. Not even to have a casual affair. Because you never could tell what would come of those casual affairs, if the girl was smart and went to work on you in dead earnest. He'd seen more than one shrewd little cutie land a swell guy on the rebound, simply because the guy was lonely and hurt and vulnerable, and therefore ripe for snatching.

And Matt wasn't having any. He'd be damned if he'd be picked off by some girl he didn't really want, simply because the girl he had wanted had given him the old double-cross. That was why he hadn't intended to stick around Kathy's room long. Maybe a few minutes. Say half an hour or so. Because, dammit, he was lonely. And his work wasn't going at all. And he couldn't remember how long it had been since he'd sat around with a cute girl and had a couple of smokes and a drink. And this Kathy really was a cute one. Cute and pretty and fiery as the dickens. The way those dark eyes of hers actually threw off the sparks when you said something that got her sore.... He wouldn't wonder a bit but what she'd be a lot of fun—for some *other* guy....

So when Kathy invited him to sit down, he said, "Okay," not too enthusiastically. But he said it. And after that, one thing led to another. Over a cigarette, Kathy told him all about that silly Henry Peterson and about how he'd kept the house upset for weeks and weeks over the baby that was due.

The way Kathy told it set Matt to laughing heartily. He really was awfully attractive when he laughed. His teeth were so white and he had such a deep, husky voice, and there was something so infectious about his laughter. He said, when she imitated Henry being so jittery about his domestic affairs, "You know, you're quite a little mimic. You have quite a knack for describing people."

Which pleased Kathy. And now that they were getting so chummy she decided to tell him about Charley Whittaker. That tale really tickled Matt no end. And he believed her story about the check. He actually believed her. "Why, sure," he said. "I can figure a guy like that coming through with a nice present. Why not?"

And that, of course, made Kathy feel very warm toward him indeed. And that reminded her that they might as well finish up that last bottle of champagne between them. Which took another hour or more. And by that time, Matt had forgotten completely that he hadn't intended to stay …

This kid was as cute as the dickens. And her eyes were so large and bright and glowing. And her mouth was so red and sweet and tempting. And he'd be a darned fool if he passed her up completely. So he sat and looked at her for quite a while, not saying a word. She had put on the scarlet jacket, but not the pajamas. And there she sat, with her beautiful legs and her hair a dark cloud framing her pert little face, and her eyes laughing into his.

Matt looked at her, and he felt the hot blood stirring in him, felt the craving which possesses the male who has been too long without the tenderness and the excitement and the passion of love, and then looks upon a girl who promises him all of these things. He thought to himself: Heck, I'd better beat it out of here. And he said to her: "Well, it's been fun getting to know you. Now I'll be running along."

But instead of going, his arm came out slowly and he drew her to him and for a moment he held her so, looking down into her uplifted face. Kathy whispered faintly, "Yes. You'd better go."

He continued to hold her. His smile was slow. "Had I?" he said. He looked down into her eyes. Dark eyes clinging to his with a kind of slow, unbelieving wonder. The kind of wonder a woman knows when an emotional miracle is coming slowly alive in her. A miracle she had not believed could happen, possibly. She moved in his arms, but the movement was not a withdrawal. He felt her tremble and he smiled.

"You want me to go?" he said.

"Yes. I—I think so."

"Sure? Very sure?"

Fire seemed to bathe her face. He saw her flushed cheeks, the quivering, moist fullness of her passionate lips. And he felt a sheer male delight; the delight of a man who sees desire slowly blossom in the woman he holds, making her more beautiful before his eyes, making her weak and trembling and vulnerable. He whispered: "You're a beautiful little devil," and then he kissed her.

And later, when he took her wholly into his arms, she made no resistance to him. Once she whispered shakily, "it must be the champagne. I didn't even like you, at first. And I don't—honest, Matt, I'm not—"

"Pshhh," he whispered. "Don't talk. Sure, I know. You don't usually. Well, I don't either. All men aren't promiscuous hounds, you know. I'm not. And it isn't the champagne, either.

It's you—me—it's one of those things that sometimes happen. Lightning striking—a man and a woman meeting who have an unholy attraction for each other. Let's not analyze it—let's just enjoy it. Lord, you're wonderful, baby. I'm mad about you. And it's been a long, long time since I've felt that way about any woman.... "

It seemed as if years had passed. And yet, in a way, it seemed only a few seconds. And now it was early morning. The first thin light seeped into the cluttered room. The candles had long since burned themselves out. Last night's party seemed like something that had happened in another life. The room was cold, and Kathy crept closer into Matt's arms for warmth. And then he was saying: "You're all a man wants, for one little night of love.... "

That seemed to jar Kathy back to reality with a dull, cold thud. She lay for a moment looking at him, and slowly, very slowly, the expression in her eyes underwent a vast change. It was as if she were gathering herself together, moving slowly and forever away from him. "So it's like that, eh?" she said.

She got up then and went to find a warm bathrobe. She wrapped herself in it and came back to sit on the edge of the couch. She lit a cigarette. It tasted foul and she made a wry face, but she went on smoking it slowly, thoughtfully.

Matt put out a lazy hand to her. His eyes were smiling. "You've changed," he said. "All in a minute you changed. You went away from me. Did I say something to make you sore?"

"Oh, no." Kathy sat and stared at the cigarette, and suddenly, there with the man so close beside her, she felt engulfed in the most terrible loneliness she had ever known. She did not understand it. Only a little while ago he had seemed so close and so dear to her. She had invited that closeness, had surrendered herself to it. And now he was like a stranger to her.

She looked at him with hard, bright eyes and she thought: That's all he is. A stranger. A man who barged in here for no reason. And she had permitted him to stay. He had things in his favor, this man. He had charm and intelligence and a kind of tenderness and a congenital decency about him toward a woman. He wasn't any bum. No doubt he was a very fine person. If they had met differently, everything might have been different between them.

They might have fallen in love. Married. Anything could have happened. But as it was—he thought her just a little tramp. And why shouldn't he? That's what she was. That's what she had turned into. And then she found herself thinking of the lovely, pleasant home where she had grown up.

It was a white frame house on the corner of a wide, tree-shaded street. There was a big porch running the width of it, with a swing and a hammock and lots of easy chairs, and the crowd used to gather there in the summer time. They were swell kids, all of them. Most of the boys had gone off to war, but some of them had married their schoolgirl sweet-hearts before they went. And the girls were established in their own little homes, having their babies, building up something that was sweet and clean and enduring for the time when their men would come back. There had been one of those boys whom Kathy might have married....

But here she was, instead, in a dismal, ugly, dirty Greenwich Village room, an attic really, with a man whom she didn't know at all, and whom she had let stay the night.

She looked around at the clutter and confusion of the room and it seemed to her that it was like the clutter and confusion and ugliness which she had created in her own life. And suddenly she began to sob, horribly....

Matt sat up worriedly. He tried to soothe her. He looked annoyed, impatient, as a man always is before the tears of a woman; tears that he cannot understand. He had no way of understanding that she was simply a girl who had been running a race, a race that was too long and too wearing for her, and that now she was tired and spent. Too tired to fight the tears off. Too tired to do anything but weep.

"What the heck's wrong?" Matt said. "Did I say something to make you go on like this?"

Kathy shook her head.

"No. It's nothing you said, Matt. Really it's not. I guess—I guess I'm crying because I'm such a darned fool."

He kept looking at her, and for a moment it occurred to him that she was putting on an act. He'd known dames to do that. They started wailing to get over the idea that they were wronged little innocents, when they'd just finished proving that there was nothing innocent about them. Sometimes they did it with the idea of framing a guy. And so he looked at Kathy with dark suspicion.

But this was no act. If it was, it was a darned good one. The kid seemed genuinely upset. He fumbled awkwardly at her arm, with some idea of quieting her tears. But Kathy pushed him away. "Don't touch me," she sobbed. "Let me alone. I'll be all right. Just let me alone."

"Look here," Matt said after a moment. "Is it because of what I said about—well, about you being nice to love for a night? You didn't think it was any more than that, did you?"

"Good heavens, *no*. Don't be silly. Why should I?"

"Well, I dunno." He shook his head. "Girls get funny ideas sometimes. There's no way for a man to figure how their minds work. I want you to know this much, kid. When I came up here, I didn't have any idea of staying. I never thought of such a thing."

"Sure, I know. I didn't think of it either."

"And then—well, things just sort of happened. I didn't want to go. And you seemed to want me to stay. But I figured you understood how it was. I didn't figure you'd take it seriously. After all, you're tied up with this other guy—"

So he knew about that. Kathy drew a long, difficult breath. She crushed out her cigarette, dabbed at her eyes. Well, what had she thought? Everybody in the house knew about her and Tommy. No doubt everyone talked about it. She said in a dead voice: "Yes, I'm tied up with this other guy."

"Are you in love with him?" Matt asked, and there was a curious intensity in his voice.

"I suppose so," Kathy said.

"What do you mean, you suppose so? Don't you know?"

Suddenly Kathy laughed, a harsh bitter laugh that had no humor or gaiety in it. "All I know for sure is that it's a lousy joke on me if I'm not in love with him."

"He lives here with you, doesn't he, Kathy?" His eyes were studying her thoughtfully.

Kathy shrugged. "That's one way of putting it. But it isn't exactly the idea. Tommy expects to write plays that will shake the world. While he's getting ready to do it, he goes around broke, cadging meals and a bed wherever he can. Well, you know how this Village crowd is. Or don't you? We don't bother much with the conventions. If a guy hasn't a place to sleep, and a girl happens to have an extra bed, she puts up a curtain to maintain the proprieties and tells the lad to go beddy-bye, until a check comes from home.... That's the way it is with Tommy. As for our being lovers—well, we fight a darned sight more than we love. Half the time we don't speak to each other. He runs around with other women, wealthy dames who go for him. I know that. Then he comes back, looking sick and discouraged and down at the heels, and I go all maternal and give him some food and put him to bed."

She laughed. "It isn't a very pretty little story, is it? But anyway, that's the way it is."

"Why don't you pull out of it?" Matt said earnestly. "A set-up like that isn't getting you anywhere, kid."

"You're telling me?"

CHAPTER TEN

Tommy came in one evening around six, and he was quite drunk. He'd been drunk, off and on now, for nearly three weeks, and Kathy was disgusted with him. Sometimes she would think: I wish he'd get rotten drunk and stay that way for such a long time that I'd be utterly sickened with him. *Cured* of him. But even while she was thinking this, another side of her mind would yearn over him with a kind of pitying love. She would remind herself: Tommy does it to escape things. Life isn't easy for a person like Tommy. He has this urge to write. He burns with it. And he does have talent. But things don't go right for him. And he never learned to fight the hardest when the going gets tough. Instead he gives up. He can't take it. But it isn't his fault....

Just whose fault it was Kathy never stopped to figure out.

She only knew that she felt darned sorry for him, and she'd do anything, anything at all, to help him get a real start.

If Tommy could just get *started*, if he could have one real success, it would make a new man of him. It would bolster his ego, give him a new grip on life, so that he could stand up and meet it like a man.

Oh, yes, she'd put up with anything to bring that about.

And that was why she was putting up with the Eunice Cairn situation, which seemed to be working up to quite a hot little tempo.

Kathy knew that Tommy was spending most of his afternoons hanging around Eunice's swanky Park Avenue apartment.

Tommy was sporting a new overcoat, and a fine, imported tweed at that. He was wearing a wrist watch. And one day he'd brought in a box containing a dozen hand-painted ties, with the name of an expensive Fifth Avenue haberdashery shop on the wrapper.

He didn't admit in so many words that Eunice was the giver of these little odds and ends. But he grinned and didn't deny it when Kathy snapped: "The dame seems to be making quite a house pet of you."

And he actually boasted of Eunice's yen for him, and of her technique as a lover. He said: "Boy, when these middle-aged sisters go for a guy, they certainly go for him."

Tommy laughed, as if he thought it terribly funny. He laughed and he laughed. "When you come right down to it," he said, "I feel sorry for a dame like that. Tied up to some thin-blooded old papa during the best years of her life. Getting more and more frustrated as time goes on. And I guess when they get past forty, they get scared stiff they'll get old and cracked up and never once know any really good loving. So it preys on their minds. And that's why, when some snappy young guy comes along, they lose control. It's sad, really."

"Very sad," Kathy agreed sarcastically. "I don't see how a woman like Eunice Cairn stands it. All those furs and diamonds and stuff, and nothing to do with them but cover her poor, frustrated little soul. Nothing to do but carry on bravely, head high, chin up, and be ever ready to make a grab for him when some guy with sex appeal makes a play for her. My heart simply weeps for her."

"Well, you don't have to be so darned sarcastic about it. Eunice has her good points."

"And I'll bet you know every single one of them by now, sonny boy. By the way, is her figure as good as mine? I should imagine, being as how she's past forty, a few of the dame's curves would be starting to slip in the wrong direction. Correct me if I'm wrong, but—"

"You don't need to be crude about it, either." And at about this point, Tommy would assume an air of injured dignity, and remind Kathy that his only real interest in Eunice was because of the help she might mean to him. "Holy Moses, you don't think I'm in love with the dame, do you? But you'd like to see me put a play over, wouldn't you? Well, I won't be the first protégé Eunice has taken on. I can name you two guys, both of them famous now, who wouldn't have got to first base if Eunice hadn't put up the dough to give them their first break. She's got a big, generous heart. And her only real interest in life is helping struggling young artists get ahead."

"Oh. I thought you said her big interest was in having a spicy love affair before it was too late."

"Well, that's just a sideline. That's what she plays at. But she *works* at the artistic angle."

"Sure it isn't the other way around, Tommy, my sweet?"

But in the end, she had to back a little water and admit there must be something in what Tommy had said, when Eunice really came through with a definite offer to put up the money, *real money*, to back a play which Tommy had started, and which she thought might be a genuine hit.

Eunice would take all the responsibility.

She knew plenty of prominent men in the theatrical world, and she guaranteed to find a producer. She would put up every cent of the cost. On a contract basis, of course. If the play was a success, Eunice would get a fifty per cent cut on all profits, and as she had told Tommy, she wouldn't be a bit surprised if she made a lot of money off of the gamble. Because she had a lot of faith in the basic idea of Tommy's play. She thought that he really had something.

And even Kathy had to admit that possibly he did have a good idea, even a brilliant one.

Tommy had called his play, *The Man Who Came Home.* And it was built around the readjustment of a returning soldier who comes home to his small town, and his small town sweetheart whom he had longed so to see again and of whom he had dreamed constantly when he was in the foxholes. But when he gets back, the little sweetheart seems quite dull and drab and the boy finds his dreams centering now around a little Hollywood lovely who had come with a show to his far Pacific island. She had been a dancer, this girl, and quite the loveliest little bit of female glamour the boy had ever seen. Anyway, she seems that way to him, now that she belongs to the past. He had talked with her for a few minutes, and she had given him an autographed picture to remember her by. And now that he is back, this picture is his dearest possession and all he can do is dream of this girl.

But the girl, of course, is really only a symbol. That was the theme of Tommy's play. She is the symbol of high adventure, of the bravery and courage of which for a little while the boy showed himself capable. Without the war, this boy would never have known anything about adventure. Doubtless he would never have left his small town. And he would surely never have had a chance to show whether he had the qualities of bravery and courage or not.

The war had given him this chance. While it was going on, it had been quite horrible, and all he had wanted was to get home. But once home, the horror no longer seemed the all-important thing. Instead, the sense of great adventure which he had known for a little while possessed him more and more. He cursed his luck, because he could not get back into the war. He cursed a life in which, in all probability, he would never again have a taste of adventurous living. He was very unhappy about it indeed. And the dancing girl from Hollywood was the symbol of all that he had known, and lost, and would never know again.

Having this dancing girl in it, Tommy felt, was a good way to get in a lot about the war, in retrospect. What the men out there had talked about when they weren't fighting Japs, or digging themselves out of slime and dirt. "I can get in a lot of good conversations," Tommy said enthusiastically. "Good, rough, man talk. I'll have two guys right down in a foxhole with bullets flying all around them, and they'll be telling each other about the last dame they had before they left for the war.... "

But right there was where Tommy hit his snag. Because Tommy had never seen a foxhole, and hadn't the foggiest idea what one was like, except what he read in the newspapers.

And Tommy didn't know how guys like that *really* talked, because Tommy hadn't been to the war. The nearest he had got to it was when he reported to his draft board, and was turned down because of a slight heart condition.

Tommy hadn't so much as given a pint of his blood, by way of the Red Cross.

Tommy, in brief, didn't know the first damn thing about the war. And as Kathy said to him once, "You might do better if you'd write a play about a man who stayed home from start to finish. You'd know something about that."

But Tommy thought the other idea was better. And so did Eunice. And as he said to Kathy, "You don't have to experience everything you write. You can *imagine* your way through it, can't you?"

So Tommy imagined his way through the first act, and it seemed to go very well. But from there on the play fell apart. He couldn't, as he said, get *into* it. He couldn't get going.

Of course, Tommy never did get past his first acts.

Kathy had never known him to. Her closet was littered with the manuscript pages of Tommy's "first acts" which refused to jell from there on.

This time he really did seem to be trying. He would sit at the typewriter for hours, muttering and cursing to himself. Or stride up and down the floor, his hair mussed, his eyes wild. Of all the bloody luck. Here, just when everything was set. The dough was waiting. A producer was practically waiting. And he couldn't get the damned thing written.

So in the end, he would slam papers down and curse his luck, and go out and head for the nearest bar.

And for three weeks now, when he wasn't up at Eunice's apartment, he'd spent most of his time in a bar getting drunk. And when Kathy scolded him about it, he would remind her that the greatest writers had sometimes gotten their best inspirations when they were liquored up. "A couple of stiff shots drive away your inhibitions," he would tell her. "They set your subconscious to work."

Kathy was not impressed. "All your subsconscious seems to do for you is tell you you need another drink. Or maybe send you toddling up to see your fancy girl friend."

Tonight when he came reeling into the room, she looked up. She had had her supper, and she was curled on the lounge reading a magazine and smoking a cigarette. "Tight again, eh?" she said pleasantly.

Tommy scowled at her. He threw off his hat and overcoat, lit a cigarette, walked over to the couch and leaned down to kiss her. Kathy pushed him away, making a grimace. That annoyed Tommy. "So you don't like my kisses these days. Every time I come near you, you push me away."

"Do I, Tommy?"

"Yes, you do. And I'm getting damned sick of it. What's the big idea? Have I become repulsive to you? Have you taken such a yen for that guy downstairs that you can't stand me near you?"

"I can't stand being kissed by a man who's drunk. Would you want to kiss me if I smelled like a walking saloon?"

"Oh. So I don't smell sweet enough. Well, isn't that too bad! Isn't that too bloody bad. Well, drunk or not, I'll kiss you when I feel like it. Understand? Just whenever I feel like it." And he caught her roughly and kissed her hard, savagely. "See?" he muttered thickly. "I'll do just as I please with you. I love you and you're mine and I don't want any funny business out of you. You'll take my kisses and like 'em. Understand?"

Kathy finally managed to push him away. She got up and went for her coat and hat. "I've got to get on the job," she said.

She'd been doing part time work, clerking behind a drug store soda fountain. She worked from seven until midnight.

"You don't have to go yet," Tommy scowled. "Funny thing. I've been noticing what a rush you are in to get off, the minute I come in. I guess that guy is going to walk you to the drug store, the way he did last night. I've got a great notion to go down and give him a good stiff punch in the jaw. He's been needing telling off. He needs to be reminded that you're my girl and he'd damned well better keep his hands off of you. I'm going to tell him so."

"I wouldn't," Kathy said sweetly.

"Why not? Ain't I got a right to tell other guys to lay off you?"

"You haven't any right to tell anybody anything," Kathy snapped. She was standing before the blurred mirror, putting on fresh lipstick. "If anybody does any telling around here, it's going to be me. And I'm telling you right now, Tommy Terry, you'd better get down to that typewriter and do a little honest to goodness work. According to your story, you've got your chance to put yourself across. Okay. Get busy and do it, or else. If you think I'm going to keep on feeding you, while you spend your days getting yourself tanked up—"

"So you're going to throw me out, eh! Kick me out like a dog. I'm trying, honey. God knows I'm trying." It was one of his lightning emotional changes. Now he threw himself down on the couch, the picture of dejection and sick discouragement. He pushed at his hair. "Can I help it if the damned play won't go right? Can I?"

"You could settle down to work. You could try."

"I have to drink, Kathy. If I don't drink I can't do anything. I tighten up inside."

"Well, you don't seem to be doing anything worth talking about, for all of your drinking. So why not try it the other way?

His eyes lifted moodily to her. "You don't think I'm any good, do you? You think I'm just kidding myself. Oh, yes, you do. I can read your mind. I know what you're thinking. You used to have faith in me, but you haven't any more. You think I'm just a lot of talk."

"Well, all you do is talk. Why don't you get to work?"

"I try, honey. Dammit, I do try."

"Well, try a little harder."

She walked over to him and put her hands on his shoulders. Her eyes were kind and gentle, loving him, mothering him. "Look, Tommy, I have just as much faith in you as I ever had. I think you have a lot of talent. You have a good mind and a flair for writing and you do think up smart ideas. But the trouble is, you won't stick at an idea until you see it through. You lose interest. You're like a child with a new toy. As long as your idea is fresh, shining bright, you're all enthusiasm. But when it gets down to the long, dull grind of keeping at it—when the newness wears off—you lose interest. You want to throw it aside for a newer and better idea. You'll never get anywhere doing that way, Tommy. You've got to learn to sit down and plug, and keep on plugging, no matter how weary you may grow of the thing. Unless you do, you'll never get anywhere. Don't you see?"

"But what's the sense in keeping plugging when it just won't go?"

"You have to learn to keep plugging, keep at it, until it does go. No one ever became successful at anything without learning to do that. You have to discipline your mind, Tommy. That's the main thing that's wrong with you. You never learned to discipline yourself. To aim at some one goal, and then keep driving yourself until you reach it. You refuse to learn. This play you're doing now—it *has* a good idea, Tommy. I think your Eunice is right. It might turn out a hit play, if it's handled cleverly. But you're just letting it fall apart. I think you've got scared of it. What are you scared of, Tommy? Failure?"

Tommy groaned, burying his face in the palms of her cool hands. "I should never have tackled it. You're right You said I didn't know anything about life in the foxholes and I don't. I'm in over my depth. I'm trying to write about something I don't know the first thing about. And I'm afraid to tell Eunice. I'm afraid to suggest something else. She might lose interest and throw the whole thing up."

Kathy thought for a moment, her eyes narrowed. "Maybe Matt Dexter could help you," she suggested carefully. "He knows all about the war. He might—well, give you a steer."

To her surprise, Tommy seemed father taken with this suggestion. He'd pretended to be so jealous of Matt, she had been half afraid to mention such a plan. And she hadn't a notion if Matt would be willing to help. But Tommy said eagerly: "Do you think he might?"

"I don't know," Kathy said warily. "I could ask him, if you want me to. Shall I ask him?"

Tommy looked up at her, interested at first. Then his eyes darkened with suspicion. "Oh, sure, you ask him. And he'll help all right. No doubt about *that*. He'll do anything you ask him. Maybe you've already asked him. I suppose the two of you have been talking me over. You telling him what a washout I am. You've probably laughed with him over my failures, made a fool of me. Maybe this is a scheme the two of you have cooked up. That guy's not dumb. Maybe he wants to show me up to you, show you what a smart guy he is."

"Oh, don't be silly," Kathy said impatiently. "I've never talked you over with Matt. And for all I know, he wouldn't waste his time helping you. He has work of his own to do, real work. And he keeps busy doing it. Forget I mentioned it."

"Don't be like that, honey," Tommy said, instantly contrite. "Don't get sore at me. It's only that I'm so jealous of you. I'm so crazy about you. I'm always afraid some guy will take you away from me. I'd be sunk if you walked out on me."

"It might be the best thing that ever happened to you if I did. Then you'd have to stand on your own two feet."

"No, honey, no. I couldn't stand it without you. I couldn't." His arms encircled her and he drew her close and snuggled his cheek against her. "I depend so on you, sweet-heart"

"You ought to stop depending on me. You should stop depending on any woman."

"Are you tired of me, baby? Is that what you're trying to tell me?"

His eyes lifted and she saw there were tears in them. This is the way he keeps his hold on me, she thought. And there was a kind of bitterness mingled with her tenderness for him.

Bitterness, for the way the man could hold her in a kind of bondage through his own weakness. You could fight a man who was tough and strong with a fiber that matched your own toughness and strength. You couldn't fight a man who lifted tearwet eyes and held your sympathy and tenderness fast with a little-boy weakness and helplessness. You simply couldn't fight that. You couldn't tell a man like that to get going and stay gone, any more than you could slap the face of a hurt kid.

"I'm not tired of you, Tommy," she said softly.

"You swear it? Do you love me as much as you ever did, sweetheart?"

"Yes, Tommy. I love you very, very much."

"And I'm nuts about you, kid. You know that, don't you?"

An odd smile curved her mouth slowly. She looked down at him and smoothed his fair hair. She did not answer.

"You won't ever leave me, will you, baby? Tell me you won't. Tell me."

She drew a long, tired breath. "How can I tell you that, Tommy? How do I know what I may do, sooner or later?"

"Then you want to leave me? You're thinking about it?"

"No."

"You lie. You act different to me lately. I've noticed it in lots of ways. It's that so-and-so downstairs. *He's* got a hold on you. You think he's hell and all because he sells his stuff. You're in love with him. You want to get rid of me. Oh, God, I won't let you go honey. I won't. Do you understand? If you try pulling out on me—"

"Do we have to go over this routine again, Tommy? I get so tired of it. Right now, I do have to go. It's quarter to seven."

"You don't have to go yet. The job will wait. Sit down here beside me, baby. Let me hold you in my arms."

"I have to go, Tommy. Now."

"You don't love me. There was a time when you wouldn't have gone. The way it used to be, all I had to do was touch you, and you forgot there was such a thing in the world as a job. And you're going to forget it now, by heaven. I'll make you forget. Baby, baby—" And he pulled her down roughly and crushed her to him and for a moment the lovely, melting feeling possessed her.

He kissed her passionately, and for a moment it was almost, *almost* as wonderful as it used to be. She closed her eyes and her senses swam and there was the illusion of dancing stars before her.

But the stars were not so bright as they once had been.

Tommy's kisses were sweet. But they no longer left her completely lost and utterly helpless against him. And she found herself thinking, strangely: Is it because I've known another man's kisses?

Suddenly, astonishingly, Tommy pushed her away from him, all but dumping her to the floor. His eyes looked savage, angry. "You've changed," he said thickly. "You don't kiss me the way you once did."

She got up slowly, pushing at her hair, smoothing her frock. "Don't be silly, Tommy."

"I'm silly, all right. But not the way you mean. I'm being played for a sucker. And I'm beginning to find it out. It used to be that you couldn't do without me. Now you just manage to endure me. Next thing, you'll be kicking me out. Well, I know when I'm not wanted. I won't stick around, waiting to be kicked out. I'll get the hell out before that happens. I'll get out now, tonight."

She looked at him for a moment; then without a word she turned and walked toward the door. She just didn't have what it took to argue with him any longer. She felt too weak, drained out. Let Tommy go, if he wanted. It would be a good way out of the whole mess.

Her small smile was thin as she ran down the stairs. But Tommy wouldn't go. Tommy hadn't the faintest idea of going. He liked to stage his little scenes. He liked to play on her sympathies. Tommy was Tommy. But he'd be right there, waiting, when she came home tonight.

He'd keep hanging on and hanging on, until maybe, some day, she wouldn't be able to take any more and something would snap in her and she really would tell him to get out, and mean it.

That was the way it would be, unless, by some miracle, Tommy really were to make a success of his play. She wondered what would happen then.

Suppose overnight, Tommy were to find himself famous and in the money. Then what? Would he really want to go on with her as he had always promised he would do? Or wouldn't he?

She sort of wished she knew the answer to that one.

CHAPTER ELEVEN

A DAMP snow was falling when Matt Dexter left the house that evening. He stopped for a moment on the steps to pull up his coat collar and tighten the muffler under it against the chill. It was a miserable night. Not so terribly cold, but raw. The rawness cut through you like a knife, and Matt's resistance was still low. He had been a gravely ill man, and it had taken its toll. He found it out on a night like this. What he should do was go south for the winter. Or maybe out to California. The doctors had suggested California. "Give yourself a winter in California while you build yourself up," the doctors had said, "and you'll be as good a man as you ever were."

Well, it was an idea. He would have to think about it.

When he had gotten the contract to do his book, he had thought that New York was the logical place to stay. A man could write better in New York, where he was in the middle of things. Where life was rushing fast and vigorously around him. Why, if he were to go out and bury himself on the West coast, he might stagnate, go to seed. All the life might ooze out of his writing. He might even lose the urge to write. Matt had heard of that happening to other writers. They got out there in California, and first thing you knew, all they wanted to do was lie around in the sun and make love to glamorous cuties.

I'll stick around little old New York, Matt had decided.

He'd work like hell and all at his book. Because this was certainly the time to do that, if he counted on making writing his profession. Now, while he had something raw and tough and real to write about, and a very real chance to make a name for himself.

Yep, he'd stay in town, and work like a son of a gun, and leave the dollies strictly alone.

That had been the agreement he had made with himself.

And it had worked out very well—until the night he had let his foot slip with Kathy Neilson.

He thought of Kathy now, and he wondered what kind of a fool he was turning into. He was forever thinking about her, and Lord knows he didn't want to. He didn't want to keep thinking about any woman. He wondered now if she would be at the drug store tonight, if he should happen to drop in there. And if she was only kidding him along when she pretended to enjoy his company. And just where things really stood between her and that good-for-nothing Terry guy.

What difference did it make anyway? Matt didn't want her. Matt hadn't any use for these screwball Village gals, playing at Art, playing at sin, playing at life. Even if there was good stuff in them, it was mostly ruined by the time they got through with messing around with their Bohemianism. Which was really only another name for going on the loose. Only they flaunted it, bragged about it, were really a little proud of it, instead of keeping it quiet, as they would have had to do in a more conventional atmosphere.

No, indeed. Kathy was the last girl, the very last, that Matt would pick out for any serious entanglement.

That's what he told himself.

He'd been saying this over and over to himself on an average of fifty times or so a day. And the oftener he said it, the more angry and confused he seemed to be. And the more unfit for the job he was trying to do.

Now he managed to get a cigarette lit and he took a long drag on it. Then, jerking his hat more closely down over his eyes, he ran down the steps and walked briskly on down the street.

He had gone about half a block when he passed a girl and a boy. The boy wore an Army uniform and the two were walking along slowly, their arms around each other. You could tell they were oblivious to everything around them. Hell, Matt thought, they didn't even know it was snowing. It might still be the middle of summer, for all those two knew or cared. No doubt they even heard little birdies singing.

There was young love for you. A form of insanity. And by the time a man came out of it, nine times out of ten he was hooked for life, and most likely to a girl who would start losing her looks and begin turning into a nagging shrew before the honeymoon was over.

Well, Matt had been lucky. He'd been through all that. And he'd come through safe and sound, still his own man. All because the girl had turned him down, of course. Which had hurt—for a time. But the hurt was over. And now that he was through it, he certainly knew his luck. It had been a mighty fine experience for him, really, just like being inoculated against some malignant disease. Because when you were through with first love, you were *through* with it.

Anyway, Matt was.

Matt wasn't the kind to walk into the same trap twice. And that, to his mind, was just what romantic love was. Simply a trap. You didn't see the girl for what she really was. There were certain qualities you were seeking in a woman, because of what you yourself were. And you attributed those qualities to some one girl who happened to attract you, you told yourself she was the embodiment of all lovely things, and you had quite a time kidding yourself—as illusion lasted.

Believe me, Matt told himself as he walked along, I've been cured. No more falling for an illusion for me, he concluded grimly.

Well, who was asking him to fall for an illusion? What was all the argument about? There wasn't anybody trying to make him fall romantically in love, was there? And if that pair of kids walking down the street were happy with each other, if there was something in their eyes even in the dim night light which hinted they were rubbing shoulders with the stars, why the devil should he care?

Where was the point in his getting sore because a boy and girl who passed him on the street were terribly in love and couldn't help showing it?

Well, Matt knew what the point was. He'd known right along. And it had to do with Kathy Neilson. He was jealous of those kids, that was the whole of it. Because they had something that was pretty wonderful. And if it weren't that he was through with all that stuff, too smart for it, he couldn't help thinking how wonderful it would be if he were that boy and Kathy were the girl with him, and they were walking along together, with their arms around each other, so crazily in love that they didn't even know it was snowing.

Only, of course, no matter how you tried, you couldn't make Kathy fit into a picture like that.

Not Kathy Neilson, the little fool who hadn't known any better, or had any more pride, than to take Tommy Terry for a lover. And who let the guy hang around and made a sucker of her.

Why, the girl was no better than a little tramp. Worse than some, really. Because lots of little tramps used their heads. When they took a boy friend, they arranged it so that they'd be getting something out of it. But Kathy—good heavens, what did she think she was getting out of it? Hanging around with that bum?

In a way, really, she deserved a lot better than she was getting. She really did. Because she was a smart kid in ever so many ways—except when it came to Tommy. She had energy and drive and plenty of ambition.

Matt had never made up his mind if she had any great talent as a dancer. But she was certainly good enough to do something with it. And she probably would have, if it hadn't been for that darned bum, forever around her neck like a millstone.

And whether she could dance or not, she certainly had the looks. She had color and animation and those wonderful eyes. And when he thought of her figure—

It was when he began to consider the intriguing curves of Kathy's figure that Matt, too, lost sight of the fact that it was snowing.

And for a moment he was as far out of this world as those two lovers he had just passed.

He was back in Kathy's room on that Saturday night, with the candles slowly flickering out, and Kathy so close and warm and sweet in his arms.

There never had been a night quite like that one. Never. Nor any woman who had possessed Matt's senses nor aroused his passion to a blazing, unquenchable heat as Kathy had done.

The beauty and the fire and the wonder of her had crept into his blood that night. And he had never been able to get her out of it.

That was the hell of it. He just couldn't get Kathy out of his blood. He couldn't get over wanting her. Except for casual meetings and talks, he had stayed away from her. He had never touched her since. But he had only to think of her, think of that night when she had lain close to him in breathless, eager surrender, when she had moved a trifle and he had felt the warmth and the softness of her trembling against him—he had only to think of these things and the madness was back in his blood. And his wanting her was a kind of torture that haunted and possessed him.

The torture possessed him now, as he crossed a street and started up toward Fifth Avenue. His hands were clenched in his pockets and he did not know it. He was muttering something under his breath to himself, and he did not realize that either until a girl passed and looked at him curiously.

She was one of the sisters of the night, plying her trade.

You had only to take one look at her to know that. But Matt didn't even see her until she sidled up to him and said softly: "You lonely, talking to yourself that way? I know a place we could go, Mister, if you'd like a little cheering up."

Matt gave her a thin smile. "No, thanks," he said. "I'm not in the mood."

After she had gone on, a kind of horror possessed him. Why, he thought, a girl like Kathy could turn into something like that. She could, for a fact Suppose she kept on and on with Tommy until the fellow tired of her and walked out Then what? The blow might be more than she could take. It might be the end of any ambition she had ever had. It might simply destroy her. Destroy all the decent things in her. Send her out either to the river or to the streets. And it was a toss-up which was the worse. The poor kid, he thought.

Matt had never considered this angle before. But now that he did consider it, and since he was rather an imaginative fellow, he became quite upset about it. He remembered a girl he had heard about a few weeks ago. She had lived in the Village for two or three years, all the time tied up to some no-good would-be artist. Well, one day the artist simply walked out. And he didn't come back. And when the girl was convinced that he was never coming back, she simply turned on the gas....

It's the unhealthy way these girls live in the Village, Matt thought worriedly. They overplay their emotions. They do that deliberately, with the idea that it releases their artistic impulses. Sometimes it was only pretense at the start. But slowly the pretense became real. They emoted all over the place. If they loved, they loved like women frenzied and possessed. If they suffered, they suffered like the damned. It became sometimes a point of pride with them to prove that no one, ever, had suffered as they did. Even if they had to turn on the gas to prove it, or take an overdose of sleeping tablets.

Something like that might happen to Kathy, Matt thought. Because he was convinced that Tommy Terry wasn't the kind of fellow who would stick by any woman, once she had served her purpose and it was more convenient for him to walk out. He would leave her flat. And as Matt thought about that, he could practically see it happening. See Kathy's helpless suffering because of it. It might be the end of everything for her. A kind of savage fury possessed Matt at the thought.

As he walked along, he imagined himself getting Tommy Terry by the throat. Feeling his fingers tighten, tighten, as they had once tightened bloatingly around the throat of a dirty, rotten little monkey of a Jap....

It did not occur to Matt at the moment that Kathy might be perfectly capable of taking care of her own emotional life. Or that she might not, after all, be so infatuated with Tommy that anything he might do would hurt her too badly.

It did not occur to him, even, that she in the end might be the one to walk out on Tommy.

And it did not seem to him that he was especially illogical, to be thinking now of Kathy as a tender, helpless little blossom who might be bruised and destroyed by the cruel hurt of love, after having told himself over and over, for days on end, that she was really not much better than a little tart, and he'd do better to leave her kind strictly alone.

He only knew that a fierce protective instinct had aroused in him, making it terribly important to him that Kathy should be saved from herself. "I'm going to have a talk with her," he told himself grimly.

More than likely she'd hate him for it.

He knew damn well you got little thanks, trying to warn a girl against a man she was mad about. As likely as not she would tell you to attend to your own confounded business. But he would have to chance it. He simply had to try to make Kathy see.

What? he asked himself suddenly. Just what is it you want to make her see?

That Tommy may leave her cold some day? And that girls have been known to take their own lives, or take to the streets, when a thing like that happens?

Well, don't you suppose she knows that already?

And you *will* sound like a darned fool, telling her about it. She'll probably laugh in your face. Who wouldn't? If you must talk, why don't you be honest about it? Say to her, "Look, kid, I don't like that guy. He gets in my hair. And if you must know, I'm jealous of him. I'm jealous as hell. Because I had you once. And I know how wonderfully sweet you are. And every time I think about him having you, any time he wants you, I nearly go out of my mind. So please, would you mind very much giving him the boot, so that I can sleep better, without being plagued with nightmares about you and him? And incidentally, so that I can get back to my work."

She'd laugh just the same, of course, if you said that.

But at least you'd make a little sense. You'd be saying something she could understand. And she wouldn't take you for a
complete idiot....

Well, anyway, Matt thought doggedly, I'm going to have a
little talk with her. A serious talk. And he headed around and
back up Fifth Avenue, toward the corner drug store where Kathy
worked.

CHAPTER TWELVE

WHEN he reached the store, he couldn't see inside for the steam on the window glass. And that reminded him again of the damp, raw night and that the chill had penetrated all through him. There was more wind now, and the snow, caught in its downward journey, was whipped back and up and into little flurries that romped around in circles in mid-air.

Matt shivered. A cup of hot chocolate, very hot, would taste good and warm him. And while he was having it, maybe he would get a chance to have a few words with Kathy. He didn't know what he would say to her. All of his fine ideas of a few moments ago about having a talk with her for the good of her soul, of her future life, or something, had abruptly gone into a tailspin.

He saw now that they made no sense at all.

He had simply been building up a fine excuse to go rushing to see her, after promising himself all day that he'd let the dame strictly alone.

It wasn't the first time he had done this.

Time and again, something would bob into his mind that it was terribly important for him to say to Kathy. He must get to her right away to say it. But when he reached her there was never anything to say, really. They talked only of the most commonplace matters.

Sometimes it seemed to him that he was a little afraid to talk to Kathy about anything real. Afraid, perhaps, of coming too close to her. And once or twice he had wondered if she was afraid of him. There was always a kind of shyness about her when she was with him. And yet she was not a shy kind of person.

He went into the store and crossed to the counter, where he found an empty stool. Some girl he had never seen before took his order, and he didn't see Kathy anywhere. This worried him. He wondered if she could be sick, and he asked the girl who brought him his chocolate, slamming it down in front of him so that some of it spilled messily over into the saucer: "Isn't Miss Neilson working tonight?"

The girl nodded. "Somebody wanted her on the phone. She'll be back in a minute."

When Kathy came, Matt saw right away that she had been crying. She looked at him and tried to smile. "Hello, Matt," she said.

Matt stared at her. "What's wrong, kid?"

Kathy looked at him and her underlip trembled. She tried to speak, but for a minute she couldn't. Then: "Babs. Girlie just called me. Fred came home about an hour ago and found Babs—"

She started dabbing at her eyes. She couldn't go on. After a time she said: "Babs was always threatening to do it. But no one took her seriously. Now—"

"How?" Matt asked.

"Something in a bottle. They found the bottle beside her, on the floor."

"Any hope?"

Kathy shook her head and her eyes filled again. Suddenly she said fiercely: "If she hadn't been such a fool about that rotten skunk. Know what he did this morning? He went all to pieces and blabbed the truth to Girlie—this morning he told Babs their marriage wasn't legal. There was another wife he'd never been really divorced from. Now he wants to go back to her, and he told Babs he was going.... "

She wiped her eyes and went down the counter to wait on a couple of customers.…

Matt hung around until ten o'clock and then he persuaded Kathy to leave for the evening. One of the other girls, who usually left at ten, agreed to stay on in her stead. Matt knew a little basement grill, just off Broadway, where they could get awfully good clam chowder. "You need something hot and nourishing," he told her.

Kathy shook her head. She couldn't eat a thing, she insisted. But she agreed to go with him. There were three small booths in the place, curtained off for privacy, and Kathy and Matt went into one of them.

For a time all Kathy could talk about was Babs.

Babs had been so terribly talented. "She was the most talented of any of us, Matt. She didn't just talk. She had the stuff. Did I ever tell you several of her pictures were on exhibit? She'd have been tops in a few years, if that damned Fred hadn't got a hold on her. She never did anything worth a hoot after she met Fred."

And again, fiercely and bitterly: "That isn't love. That's madness. When a woman completely loses her perspective. When a man gives her nothing but unhappiness, when he sponges on her, abuses her, humiliates her before everyone, and she knows it, and yet she hangs on. And in the end kills herself rather than live without him.

"A woman like that should be locked up somewhere until she comes out of it."

And Matt said quietly: "I quite agree." But it wasn't until after they'd finished the chowder and then ordered coffee to have with their cigarettes that he gave her an odd look and asked: "Are you quite sure you aren't suffering from the same disease that proved fatal to Babs?"

"You mean Tommy?" Kathy looked at him, and she laughed a little. "No. Anyway, I haven't it in any such advanced form, I can promise you that. I can't see little Kathy taking poison over Tommy." And she couldn't.

In some indefinable way—she hadn't had time to analyze it—the tragedy of Babs had helped to crystallize her feeling for Tommy. It wasn't exactly that she identified herself with Babs, or Tommy with Fred. And yet—that old line flashed across her mind: "There, but for the grace of God, go I." And she thought: There was a time, and not so long ago, when I would rather have died than do without Tommy.

The thought sent a little chill through her. And then a feeling of freedom, wonderfully light, poured through her. It was as if she had thrown off a burdensome shackle, as she reminded herself: I *still* love Tommy, but not the way I once did. Not enough for *that.*

She thought: If Tommy were to walk out on me this very night, I'd get over it. But she did not know that in telling herself that, she was in truth admitting that her infatuation for Tommy had already begun its inevitable death.

Suddenly she heard her own laughter and it sounded quite gay. "Oh, no," she said, "don't worry over me, Matt. I'm not the type that goes around calling it quits over any guy."

"Sure about that?"

"Quite sure."

"Would that mean, by any chance, that you're fed up with Tommy?"

"No." she thought for a minute. "I don't think so. Anyway, I'm still terribly fond of him. I'd do anything to help him be successful." And that reminded her of Tommy's play and her suggestion that Matt might be willing to help him over the rough places.

"Would you?" she said, when she had told him how things stood. "I suppose I have an awful nerve suggesting it to you. I don't really know you well enough to ask any real favors of you. And this is such a big favor. Maybe it's preposterous, asking one writer to do another man's stuff for him." She smiled at him. "Only it never hurts to ask, does it?"

"No," Matt said quietly. "It never hurts to ask."

He studied her for a minute, not speaking. Then his hands came across the small table, seeking hers. He took them, holding them palms up, in his own. He looked at them; he played with her fingers. His eyes, strangely dark, thoughtful, came up to hers.

"So you'd like me to write his damn play for him," he said finally. "Well, you're right, kid. That's asking quite a lot. And you have your pride. It must hurt your pride to ask me to do a thing like that for your boy friend. Why do you do it?"

Kathy felt her cheeks flush crimson under his gaze. "Well—I—oh, you know why I'm doing it."

"No. I don't quite know. Are you sure that you know?"

"Of course. I'm so terribly anxious for Tommy to succeed. He has talent, Matt. Really he has. Only—well, I feel if he could just get a start, have one real success—"

"I see. Tommy just must get his one success. It's so important to you that you're willing to do anything, anything at all—even to asking favors of other men—to get his success for him."

His voice had been quiet, even cold, but suddenly it turned angry and his eyes were savage. "And how much are you willing to *pay* for that success—to get it for your lover?"

Her hands shrank away from him, and her face blanched. "Matt! And I thought you were a decent sort of guy. I trusted you to understand, to take that the way I meant it."

"Sure you did. And that's just what I am doing, taking it the way you meant it. You want me to write the guy's play for him.

And I assume you're prepared to make me an offer. Okay. Go ahead and make it, and I'm likely to take you up on it." His eyes blazed on her face, and his arm, as he slipped around to the cushioned seat beside her and held her, was shaking.

For a moment, the hatred that Kathy felt toward him was a choking, horrible thing. I must get out of here, she thought; get away from him. She never wanted to see the man again.

But she had no power to move, and she endured his arm around her, and her eyes, held to his face, saw his sudden complete change of expression. She saw his eyes soften, saw his slow twisted smile. "Forget I said that, will you, honey? I'm pretty nuts about you, kid. Too much so for comfort. And it gets me down when I see the limits you'll go to for that guy. I'm jealous, I guess. And you have to make allowances for a jealous guy."

Kathy frowned at him. "You don't make sense, Matt. Why should you be jealous of Tommy? I'm nothing to you. I'm just a girl you had an hour of fun with, one night when we were both a little tight. You told me that yourself. You were pretty careful I shouldn't get any wrong ideas about it, or take you seriously. Remember?"

Yes, Matt remembered. He drew her closer and his eyes were angry again, his voice thick. "That's what I said. And that's what I mean. A little fun. That's all I want with any girl, understand? I'm not falling in love with any dame. Not now I'm not. That's not part of my schedule. But, damn you, I can't get you out of my mind, you little witch, you. I think about you all the time. I even dream about you. And I'm the kind of a guy, when he starts dreaming about any dame, he's in bad shape. I've tried to let you alone. I don't want to waste my time making a play for a tootsie who's tied up to some other guy."

"Maybe I'm not as tied up to Tommy as you think." Kathy's voice was faint, unsteady. Her eyes in his glowed strangely.

He leaned over then and kissed her lips, and his mouth against hers was alive with his need of her, brutal, hurting. She felt the hurt of it, and found it sweet and lovely.

"Don't hand me that line," he muttered. "Either you're tied up to him, or you aren't. And it's perfectly plain that you are. But just the same, I'm crazy about you. I haven't had enough of you. I can't get you out of my mind, or my blood, and heaven knows I've tried. Heaven knows I want to. So now you come to me and you want me to do a favor for *him*. Okay. I'll do it."

"You will, Matt? You will? Oh, that's wonderful." Her eyes widened and she managed a smile, but she wasn't really thinking much of what she had said. With Matt's arm around her, with the pain of his kisses still branded on her lips, it wasn't easy to think, or to care very much, about the success of Tommy's play.

"Yes." Matt said thickly. "I will. I'll make a bargain with you."

"A bargain, Matt?"

"Yeah." And he laughed harshly. "You didn't think this was all to be for free? I want to see more of you. I want to come to see you whenever I feel like it. I want to talk with you. I want to sit around and laugh and eat and joke and get tight with you. I want to make love to you. I want you for *my girl*—for a couple of weeks. Then maybe I'll be able to get you out of my system. Then maybe, by the end of that time, I'll be sick of the sight of you, and I'll be able to get back to work and get on with my life like a sane guy ought to do."

"That's a funny kind of a proposition."

"Funny or not, that's my proposition," Matt said. He seemed to be getting more and more angry. He was like a man torn to pieces by some inner conflict.

"You send Tommy off somewhere else to do his sleeping—"

"But where?" Kathy inquired logically. "Tommy hasn't any place to go. And he hasn't any money. His family used to send him checks every month, and that's what he lived on. But it's been nearly two months now since one came. That's why he's been parking in my place. And I just didn't have the heart to turn him out."

"I don't care where the devil he sleeps," Matt said savagely. "Let him sleep on a park bench. And it probably wouldn't kill him instantly to go to work and earn an honest dollar. Anyway, get him out. Clear the place out so I can come up and see you when I feel like it. You do that, and I'll write his damn play for him. And if he makes a fortune on it, it's all his.

"Only your time has got to be all mine."

"And how long is this extraordinary arrangement to last?" Kathy asked faintly.

He held her and looked at her for a moment, and then he started kissing her again. "Until I'm tired of you," he whispered huskily. "Until I'm ready to walk out and say, Well, so long, kid, it's been fun knowing you.' Until I can do that—and not give a damn."

CHAPTER THIRTEEN

K ATHY was back in her room on a Saturday afternoon.
Kathy was back in the black satin gym trunks.

Kathy was back exactly where she had been when she first came to New York. At least, so she was telling herself as she tap danced with a kind of fury on the bare, unpainted, wooden floor.

Just exactly nowhere, she told herself bitterly. That's where I've got. And she had no one to blame but herself.

If she'd stuck to the original idea, which had been to make a famous dancer of herself. If only she'd done that! But no. She'd had to go into an emotional tailspin over Tommy Terry. And then Matt Dexter had come along, and while she had never believed and still didn't believe that you could be in love with two men at the same time, she had to admit that Matt hadn't simplified her emotional problems. And now—

Well, now, as far as she could make out, both of them had taken a powder.

The worrying she had done about how to get rid of Tommy as a non-paying guest, without hurting his poor little feelings, or bringing on a stormy jealous quarrel.

She had actually lain awake one solid night, trying to figure out how to do the thing tactfully. I'll tell him a cousin is coming to New York on a visit, she decided finally, and that I need my extra couch. If the worst came to the worst, she might actually stir up some relative who would come. She thought of several other plausible lies, too. But the cousin story seemed the most convincing.

And then, as it turned out, she hadn't needed any story at all. Because Tommy came to her and announced that he was leaving. Well, for a week or so anyway. Maybe permanently. He couldn't be sure as yet. And when Kathy looked at him, round-eyed, and asked: "Good heavens, Tommy, don't tell me you have a *job*," he had been slightly indignant over the slurring implication.

But not too indignant. He had smiled patiently, a little like a man who deserved any unkind things she might say to him. "As a matter of fact," Tommy said rather loftily, "I do have a temporary job. Chauffeuring," he added vaguely. And he went on quickly, before she could pin him down with questions:

"I've been doing a lot of thinking, Kathy. I've realized suddenly that I've allowed you to do too much for me. Far too much." He shook his head thoughtfully. "You're a damn swell little kid, honey. No two ways about that. You've stood by me when most women would have kicked me out long ago. But that's the sort you are. Loyal to the last ditch. And don't think I don't appreciate it, kid. Don't you ever think that for one minute. But there comes a time when a man simply can't take any more favors from a woman, and I've reached that point. I—well, I just can't hang around here any longer. I simply can't do it. I realize I'm not pulling my share of the load, and it isn't fair to you, and that's why I'm pulling out. Anyway, temporarily."

This doesn't quite make sense, Kathy thought. And somehow Tommy wasn't being very convincing.

It was a fine line of talk, but somehow out of character. It simply wasn't like Tommy to have a sudden attack of conscience or a sudden urge to take on his share of the responsibility. Not unless there was something behind his big talk that she hadn't guessed.

Well, she wouldn't doubt but what she could make a couple of guesses and come up with the right answer, if she tried hard enough. She had an awfully strong hunch that Eunice Cairn fitted into the puzzle somewhere. Chauffeuring, he had said. Well, possibly Eunice was making a trip some where and thought it would be a cute idea to take Tommy along.

And that guess spoke awfully well for Kathy's hunches.

She said to him: "But, Tommy, this is a queer time for you to—well, sort of disappear out of the picture. Just when Matt has agreed to help you with your play. Have you lost interest in the play? Don't tell me you've given it up. After I swallowed my pride and went to Matt—"

Oh, no. *No.* Tommy hadn't for a moment given up the play. But he'd run up to see Matt last night and had a little talk with him. And Matt thought he could do more effective work on it if he was left to himself. "I've explained the idea to him," Tommy said. "And I've turned over to him all the work I've done up to date. Of course, when you come right down to it, all the real work is done. All Dexter has to do, really, is polish it off."

"The real work done?" Kathy stared. "Why that's nonsense, Tommy. You haven't even finished one act. And do you mean to tell me you're dumping the whole job on Matt? You aren't even going to come in every day and collaborate with him?"

Tommy shrugged. "He doesn't want any collaborating. He told me to leave the play with him, and then get the hell out and leave him alone. Anyway," Tommy said airily, "the only thing of real value in a job like this is the *idea*. And the idea is mine. Writing the thing is just routine stuff. Anybody could do it."

"Sure," Kathy agreed scornfully. "Anybody could write it! Anybody, maybe, except *you*. And after all, why should you waste your time *writing* plays, when you can get one girl friend to persuade another man to write it for you, and another girl friend to put up the dough? When you can work it that way, you'd be pretty silly to settle down to the drudgery of grinding it out for yourself." She was so strangely keyed up and blind with outraged anger for a moment that for the first and only time she told him the ugly truth about himself.

"The truth is, as a playwright you're a darned fine panderer."

The quarrel that followed, naturally, was an ugly one.

One of their best. And before they had made it up, before there was time for Tommy to coax Kathy back into his arms, according to his usual routine, Tommy had to go.

As he put it: "I'm getting out of here. I won't be talked to like that, see? No dame, not even you, can talk to me like that and get away with it. The truth is, and don't think I don't see through you, you're in love with that Dexter guy. That's why all of a sudden I'm just a heel. Well, okay, be in love with him. You'll soon get your fill of him. You'll be glad enough to get me back. But don't be too sure I'll come running, after the way you just talked to me. There's such a thing as going too far, even with a guy who's been as nuts over you as I've been. Just think that over. Think it over while I'm gone, baby."

And then he really had gone, and he hadn't been back since. Which hadn't worried Kathy too much. She was a little sorry about the way she had talked to him. Maybe she had gone too far. Although Tommy certainly had it coming. But she wouldn't worry. Tommy would be back. When he needs me for something, she thought grimly.

And besides, now she had Matt to worry about. Just what had she let herself in for, promising Matt to get Tommy out of the picture? Telling Matt he could have the free run of her apartment? ...

He'll think I'm just a cheap, promiscuous little tramp, she reminded herself. He'll take me for one of those miserable little weaklings who take orders from any man who comes along. And she didn't want Matt to think that about her.

She wanted him to believe she was a girl with some pride, and to know that she *wasn't* promiscuous. That except in the case of Tommy, who had really been a kind of delirious fever that she had no power to fight off, she was at heart as conventional and strait-laced as you could imagine.

She wanted him to know all this, because—well, because that was the way she really was. But how in the world could she expect him to believe it?

And why, *why* had she ever promised him all he'd asked the other night? About getting Tommy out of the picture. About letting Matt come up whenever he felt like it. She hadn't, of course, realized quite what she was saying, she had been so upset and emotionally torn because of Babs. And then, there was just something about Matt which made her lose all her reasoning powers when she was around him.

Of course, too, she had been excited over his promise to help Tommy out with his play. There had been everything taken together. Not forgetting that Matt had had her in his arms when she had made her promise. And when Matt held her close to him, when he started kissing her, she simply didn't know what she was saying. That night it had been a little like going into a trance. And when she came out of it and began to figure exactly what she had let herself in for—

Well, she didn't like the picture. She didn't like the interpretation Matt would put on it. That she was the kind of a gal who would promise a man anything.

And she worried and worried, wondering how in the world she was to convince Matt that she had dignity and pride, and that while she was glad to be friends with him, it simply couldn't be more than that.

And if she did convince him, he'd most likely get sore. He'd accuse her of being a welcher on her bargain, and maybe wash his hands of Tommy's play. And—oh, any way she looked at it, it was a mess, a complete mess. She bad a great notion to run away some place. Go back home. What was the sense in her hanging on in New York, anyway? She wasn't doing a darned thing with her dancing, and probably never would. The truth was, she'd almost lost interest in becoming a dancer. Which was just a sample of what happened to a girl when she got mixed up with a lot of darned men.

You wanted to be a dancer. So you met a man. And then you met another man. And the next thing, you didn't know where you were at. You were just a battlefield for a lot of conflicting emotions, pulling you one way and then another. And deep down in all the raging turmoil of your inner being, there was a still, desperate little voice forever trying to make itself heard: I want Matt to believe I'm on the level. I want that more than anything!

Oh, Matt, she thought, I've got to make you understand.

I've simply got to. I've never told you much about myself, have I, Matt? What kind of a girl I was before I came to New York. What my home was like, how I grew up, how I was always something of a little prig, really. Until I came here and started living in the Village. I must explain to you that maybe it was this Village life that was too much for me. People talking about their lovers and their unconventional ways of living. Boasting about it. Looking *down* on a girl who hadn't a single lover. Sort of sneering at her. Making a kind of pariah of her. Making her feel that she simply couldn't expect to really *belong*, until she'd dished herself up at least one little slice of unconventional living.

That's the way it was, Matt. Maybe you can't understand it, but I'm telling you the truth. I'll always remember a girl back home, Matt, who 'went to the bad,' as they called it there. She had a baby, with no visible father or sign of a wedding ring, and she was simply ostracized. Finally she left town Mostly, I guess, because she must have been so terribly lonely, with everyone ignoring her, sticking up their noses at her.

Well, believe it or not, Matt, that's the way a girl can be made to feel in the Village, only in reverse. If you haven't taken a lover, and preferably several of them—if you haven't *lived*, as they call it—they simply haven't any time for you. They call you provincial, small-town. Some girl said that to me, Matt. She said: "Why, you're just a little small-town provincial, aren't you? You don't belong in the Village." She was kind to me, in a pitying kind of way. But she didn't want to be bothered with me. None of them wanted to be bothered with me, at first.

Maybe you think I'm just building up an alibi for myself, Matt. I guess it sounds that way. But truly, I'm only trying to tell you how it really was. How *lonely* I was, at first, and how desperately, desperately I wanted really to belong to this crowd of writers and artists of one sort and another. At first they seemed such wonderful, wonderful people to me. I thought they were doing such grand big things. Because they all said they were. And I believed them. At first I did. Before I discovered that most of them were phonies.

And I was discouraged about my dancing. I didn't seem to be getting anywhere at all with it. So I was a little desperate about that, too. And some of them said to me, "You'll never get anywhere as a dancer, you'll never get anywhere in any artistic line, until you've *lived*. Because," they said, "dancing, acting, all artistic expression is largely emotional expression. And until you've learned to give way to your emotions how on earth can you expect to get anywhere?"

They said: "What you need, honey, is a lover."

And then, of course, Tommy came along. And I really did fall for him. It was just one of those things. But there it was. And living in the Village had torn down all the defenses I might have had against him. There was no use in telling myself it was wrong, or even foolish and cheap. Because all these weeks and months I'd been listening to their talk. And they said it was simply too silly not to. They said: "How lucky for you that Tommy came along. He's just what you you've been needing, honey. An affair with Tommy will bring you out."

So that's how it was, Matt. That's how I drifted into it. I don't know why I'm telling you all this, except that—well, I just wanted you to know.

She would tell him all this. And maybe, just maybe, it would help him to understand her a little better. Make him more tolerant of what must seem to him the very sordid set-up of her love life. She went over and over it in her mind, deciding just how she would put certain things.

Only the trouble was, she never had a chance to tell Matt any of these things. Because a solid week had passed, and a few days over, and there hadn't been a sign of him.

Matt had never come near her. And she had about lost hope that he was ever going to. The way it looked, Matt had simply dropped her cold.

The first day or so, she had simply wondered. Maybe, while he was getting into his stride with the play, he didn't want to talk to anyone. Writers were like that, she knew. While they were getting into the feel of a new job, they liked to be by themselves.

Then she began to worry.

And finally, now, she was good and sore. The way it looked, he had simply been testing her out, making a kind of a fool of her. Telling her to throw Tommy out, just to find out if he could make her do it. And afterwards, no doubt, laughing to himself because she had agreed.

Well, she was tempted to march downstairs and spoil his little smug moment of triumph by telling him that Tommy's leaving had been none of her doing. That Tommy's leaving had been strictly his own idea.

She'd certainly like to tell him that. And she had a great notion to go and do it. Only she would never be able to bring herself to go near the man. Never. And if he thought she was going to come running after him, he certainly had another think coming.

Men, she thought furiously, as her feet tapped over the floor like clicking castanets.

They thought they were hell and all. They thought they could treat a girl just as they pleased. Pick her up, set her down, use her for an easy mark, walk out on her when it pleased them to do it. Well, the heck with them. She was through with the lot of them. If Tommy Terry ever came crawling back to her, she'd tell him to get going, and fast.

And as for Matt Dexter—her breath came with angry difficulty at the very thought of the man. She doubted, she very much doubted, if she would so much as speak to him if she were to pass him on the stairs. She would simply give him a haughty stare, and if he tried to speak to her, she would hold her distance as if she were very much afraid that she might be contaminated by the very touch of his coat sleeve. And maybe she would say frigidly: "Pardon *me*, but have we met somewhere before? Your voice sounds familiar, but I don't quite remember the face."

It was very heartening to her, visualizing this possible scene. Oh, she'd let him know how little concerned she was with him. She'd give him to understand that she'd completely forgotten him. Try to make a sap of her, would he? Well, just let *any* man try that again.

From now on, men were out, as far as she was concerned. She was going back to her dancing. She'd take up her lessons again. Next week, in fact the first thing Monday, she'd make arrangements about that. And she'd work, really work. So many hours every day, not just by fits and starts. She'd give it everything she had for—well, say six months. And after that—

She never did get around to planning beyond that six months' probation period, because just then someone knocked. And when she went to the door, it was Charley Whittaker.

The mild little banker stood there, smiling genially, his eyes kind behind his heavy-lensed spectacles. "I don't suppose you remember me," he said in his almost shy way.

"Why, of course I remember you, Mr. Whittaker." She was a little surprised to see him, but not too surprised. So many curious things had been happening lately, she was past being astonished at anything.

"Do you mind if I come in?" he said. "I was strolling around and I happened to find myself near here and—well, it just occurred to me to drop in and see how you were getting along."

"Well, I'm awfully glad you did," Kathy lied. "I'm glad you remembered me." She led the way into the room, took his hat and coat. Then, with a funny little laugh: "If you'll excuse me a minute—" she looked down at the brief dancing trunks which exposed her slim, lovely legs—"I'll go cover up a bit. You always seem to see me, Mr. Whittaker, when I'm underclad."

"But I like you that way." And Charley smiled. "Please don't cover up on my account. After all, I'm just a harmless old fellow. And you're so pretty just as you are."

"Suppose I take cold?" Kathy suggested archly.

Charley winked at her naughtily, as he retrieved his top-coat for a moment and fumbled in the pocket. He came up with a quart bottle of Scotch. Pre-war Scotch. He showed her the label proudly. "Look at that," he said. "It's a bottle I've been saving."

Kathy's eyes rounded. "Oh, Mr. Whittaker. That's marvelous. I don't know when I've seen anything like that. But you aren't going to waste it on *me!*"

Charley gave her an odd, sidewise glance as he fumbled at the seal with a pocket knife. "I hope it won't be wasted, my dear," was all that Charley said for the moment.

CHAPTER FOURTEEN

C HARLEY WHITTAKER would have denied hotly that he had come to see Kathy that day with carnal thoughts in mind. And up to a point, he would have been telling the truth. He most certainly did not say to himself, as a cruder, and possibly younger man might have done: "I think I'll run up and see if I can make the dame." As a younger man, it had not been his habit to deal altogether frankly with the appetites and yearnings of the flesh. He had never quite learned to call a spade a spade, even in his own mind.

And now that he was getting old, it seemed too late for him to learn. Instead, he fell back on the device of telling himself little fairy tales, so to speak. If the thought of a pretty pair of legs possessed him, bringing lecherous desires in its trail and a concurrent sense of guilt, Charley would tell himself: "My, there's a fine, lovely, sweet little girl. What a shame if she ties herself down to marriage with some dull, unappreciative fellow, before she's ever had a real chance to better herself."

Precisely what Charley gained by this form of self-delusion was not quite clear, even to himself. But somehow it made him feel better, more the honorable gentleman about the whole thing. And if some thing in the nature of a little intrigue happened to develop, with the girl playing Charley for all he was worth, and with Charley playing the gullible and generous angel, Charley could always justify himself with the thought: There was more to it than just sex. A great deal more. I really wanted to help the girl....

For some years now—until the day when Kathy's well planned curvaceousness swam before him in Yvette's Fifth Avenue salon—there had been very little dallying in Charley's life. There had been too many other things to worry about. The war, for instance, which disturbed Charley no end. And of course, taxes. Then there was his health. He had worried and stewed over taxes and government regulations until, for a time, he was all but unable to eat. Which in turn had caused the doctors to warn him that if he didn't stop worrying and fussing his stomach might go back on him completely, and he'd be finished.

This caused Charley to start taking a desperate interest in the news items concerning the untimely deaths of active business men around his own age. He took an almost morbid interest in these deaths. And more than once he said to himself: Why, my God, I might go off myself, any day.

The net result was that he worried more frantically than ever, which left him with practically no strength or energy for the more pleasurable worry over luscious women. Which was about where matters stood with Charley on the first day that Kathy met him.

Since then, however, a slow and subtle change had crept into Charley's thinking. He found himself approaching the problems of his life—of his life and death, you might say—from a somewhat different angle. He found himself wondering: "Well, now, if I'm likely to kick off any time, don't I owe myself a little fun before it happens? Just one more little whirl at the pleasurable things of life?"

It seemed, in all justice to himself, that he did.

The truth was, of course, that he couldn't get Kathy out of his mind.

It was unacceptable to his reason, however, to say to himself frankly: "Look, brother, you're just an old coot who's gone overboard for the curves of a cute little model. And that's okay. There's fun to be had there, maybe, so go to it. But don't kid yourself as to what this is all about."

No, Charley simply could not face such a situation with such crude abandon. And so, as usual, he rationalized.

He said to himself: Now there's a mighty fine little girl who deserves a helping hand. She wanted to be a dancer, and it seemed to him there was no question but what she was a good dancer. A very lovely one, and talented. Extremely talented. She certainly did deserve a boost up, if any girl ever did. He admired her courage and her ambition, her determination to get ahead despite all obstacles. And if a man in his financial position came on a brave little girl like that, struggling so fiercely in the face of discouragement, the least he could do, the very least, was to put out a helping hand.

This had been his mood, now, for some weeks. It was his mood on the Saturday afternoon when he came up to see Kathy. He had been tempted to come any number of times before but had always managed to talk himself out of it. Now, however, on this particular day, he came to some sort of a vague decision.

I'll just drop in and see how she's getting along, he said to himself. The idea even suggested itself that she might be ill and have no one to look after her. Perhaps not even able to afford a doctor. He had a vague notion that these Villagers were never able to afford even the scant necessities of life. And he could never forget that he, in an indirect way, had been the cause of Kathy losing her job in such an unfortunate way. He was forever haunted with a sense of guilt when he remembered this, and it gave him the feeling that he was more or less responsible for her.

Yes, indeed, it was little enough for him to drop in and make sure she was getting along all right.

And so, up to a point, it was with the noblest intentions that Charley rapped at Kathy's door that day. And that nobility stayed with him straight through their second high-ball, and until they were well into their third....

Up to this point their conversation had been on a quite innocuous level.

Kathy produced glasses and a bottle of ginger ale, and while she was so engaged, Charley fired up the little pot-bellied stove. It amused him to do this. He said that the stove reminded him of one in the little parlor of the old farmhouse where he was born. It brought back fond memories of his boyhood. And when Kathy said politely that she would love to hear more about his boyhood, Charley was quite pleased. There was nothing he enjoyed better than living over the days of his youth. The struggles, the hardships, the shivering cold when he had to be up at daybreak to milk the cows; the cozy Saturday nights in the old farm-house kitchen when the boys, he and his three brothers, would have their baths in a great tin tub which his mother brought in from the back porch.

So they sat on the couch, side by side, with their high-balls, while Charley told her about these things. And he couldn't help thinking what a little darling she was. The interest she showed! Her cute little giggle, the way her eyes lighted up with laughter, when he told her about that old tin bathtub. Because it seemed to amuse her so much, Charley made quite a story out of it.

During the second highball, Charley brought the situation a bit more up to date. He smiled at Kathy and took her hand. Warily, at first, as if he were half afraid to touch her. As if her warm, smooth little fist were a firecracker that might go off under a too abrupt approach.

When nothing of the sort happened, however, he seemed to gain confidence. His pressure over her fingers tightened. "Well," he said, "how have you been, little girl?"

"Oh, I've been fine, just fine. How have you been?"

"I've been very well. Very well indeed. I've been thinking a lot about you," he added daringly.

"Really?"

He nodded. "I certainly have. I've thought quite a lot about you. Have you thought about me?"

The truth was, of course, that she hadn't. But it wouldn't be very polite to say so. She smiled brightly at him. "Of course I've thought about you, Charley. My goodness, how could I ever forget you, after your kindness to me? That wonderful, wonderful check. I don't believe I've ever thanked you properly for that."

"I don't want thanks, little girl. It was a pleasure to give it to you. By the way, did you buy yourself something pretty with it?"

To which Kathy replied unexpectedly: "I put most of it in the bank. I thought it would be a good idea to have that money in case of a rainy day."

In a sense, nothing could have pleased Charley more. There was nothing that aroused his admiration more than a girl who had the sense, the foresight, to realize that sooner or later there would come a rainy day. And he had encountered so few women, in the course of his life, who felt that way about it.

And yet he seemed a trifle crestfallen, slightly disappointed. "I wanted you to enjoy that gift," he said. "I wanted you to blow yourself to something you'd always wanted and never had."

"Well," Kathy grinned, "that's just what I did. I've never had several hundred dollars ahead before. It's an awfully nice feeling to have it." Then she added, "I'm going to start in with my dancing lessons again. I'll use some of it for that."

Charley's hand continued to tighten over hers. His eyes, through the heavy lenses, looked at her with unbounded adoration. "What a wonderful little girl you are," he said. "Smart, ambitious, sensible." He sighed. "There aren't many girls to equal you, Kathy. You deserve the best that life has to offer, the very best." He sighed again. "I wish I could help to give you the best," he said sadly.

"Oh, but you have helped," Kathy said. "You were terribly generous. I didn't," she added, "feel that I should accept that check from you. But I was afraid your feelings might be hurt if I returned it."

"I would have been hurt," said Charley earnestly. "Very deeply hurt. It was only a friendly gesture. I wanted you to feel that I was your friend. You do feel that I'm your friend, don't you, little girl?"

"Oh, yes. You're a wonderful friend, Charley."

"Good. *Good.* That's just the way I want you to feel: that I'm your real, good, kind friend. If you're ever in trouble I want you to feel you can call on me. You'll remember that, won't you?" He patted her leg gently, whereupon Kathy began to squirm a trifle.

"Oh, yes," she said. "I'll remember. Only—" she smiled teasingly—"I'll remember just as well without any little pats to help the idea to sink in."

"Now, now." He finished the third highball and smiled at her. He decided to remove his glasses, and he did so and laid them carefully on the little table. He said that it sometimes rested his eyes to take them off.

By the middle of the fourth highball Kathy really didn't care when Charley slipped his arm around her. She wasn't in the least thrilled, but she wasn't especially annoyed, either. She thought: I'll let this situation develop a bit. Then when I'm old, I can brag that once upon a time a wealthy New York banker—

Charley said: "Oh, Kathy, you're so beautiful. You're really the loveliest child. When I hold you in my arms I get so excited. I scarcely know how to tell you. You're so little, so soft, you—you make me feel like a boy again." This was quite a little later, and Charley's face had grown very flushed. His cheeks looked swollen, somehow. And his eyes looked smaller, and a little glazed. He said, leaning over her: "Kathy, do you know what an angel is?"

Kathy giggled, running her fingers through his thinning hair. "You mean the kind of angels that prowl Broadway and sometimes send little showgirls scooting up into the bright lights?"

Charley nodded. "That's the kind I mean, little girl."

"Are you somebody's angel?" Kathy asked.

"No," Charley said. "But I'd like to be. I'd like to be your angel Kathy, you have a lot of dreams about becoming a famous dancer. Maybe I could make all those dreams come true. Will you let me do it?"

He went on hoarsely: "I'm getting along in years, little girl. The sands are running out. And I have more money than I know what to do with. When I die, what's left will go to my wife, who's led me the devil of a life, and to her greedy relatives, who no doubt spend their days praying that I'll be taken off with a heart stroke. I'd like to spend some of it on someone I really care about—before I die. I'd like to spend it on you. I'll make a successful dancer of you, Kathy. I'll back a play—people often come to the bank to borrow money for such things. I have one in mind right now. A Mrs. Cairn has been after me to loan her the money for such a project: I'll put up the money, on condition that a big dancing part is written into it. And you will have that part. That's how easily it can be done. And I'll do it for you, little girl. If you'll let me. If you'll be kind to me.… "

Kathy was staring at him oddly. "What did you say that woman's name was? The woman who wants to borrow money for that play?"

"A Mrs. Cairn," Charley said carelessly. "Eunice Cairn. Well, what about it, little girl?" His arms came closer around her, crushing her. And for a moment his eyes looked oddly blank with the intensity of the need which drove him.

Charley was enjoying the soft warmth of a lovely woman for the first time in he didn't remember how long. And he was beside himself with the agony of loveliness it aroused in him. Why, he thought to himself: I'm not old. I'm not old at all. I'm as young as I ever was. Only a man in whom young blood still stirred could feel such rapturous delight. He thought crazily to himself: I'd like to take her away some place and live with her for the rest of my days. We could run away—we could simply disappear. I could arrange for my wife's future, leave everything in order at the bank, and then simply walk out. Men had done that before. They had left their families and their businesses and walked out, and never been heard of again.

If other men had done it, why shouldn't he do it?

Life was short at best, and the greater part of his was over. And once you were in the grave, you were there from then on. So why shouldn't he enjoy the little more time that was allotted to him? Why shouldn't he make the most of it?

The very thought of all this blissful stretch of heaven regained—by which he really meant youth regained—sent Charley into a perfect frenzy of amorous intensity.

He kissed Kathy and kissed her until she became a little alarmed. The guy is getting just a little too hectic, she thought. She would never have believed it of him. She had intended only to kid him along a little. Then that little announcement about his being Eunice Cairn's banker had startled her so that for a few moments she scarcely noticed what he was doing.

Now she caught herself up and attempted to push him away. "Now look, Charley," she said chidingly. "Fun's fun, and all that. But there's such a thing as going too far. Don't you go too far, Charley."

But Charley had already gone too far in his thoughts to be stopped. He said thickly: "Kathy, I'm in love with you. I'm mad about you. I haven't felt like this over any woman in thirty years."

She tried to smile, to keep things on a joking plane. "Now look, chum, get hold of yourself. Put on the brakes. You aren't in love with me and it's silly to say so. Look, let's you and I have one more little drink—just as good pals—and then you run along, eh?"

"You don't take me seriously. But I *am* serious. I was never so serious in my life. Kathy, will you go away with me?"

"Go away with you?" She laughed. She supposed that he meant for a playful week-end, and she said lightly: "Nope, brother. I'm not one of the week-end sisterhood."

"I'm not talking about any week-end. I want to take you away forever."

"Forever?"

"Well, for the rest of my life," said Charley, narrowing the thing down a bit. "I want to take you away and live with you. If I can get a divorce, I'll get it. If I can't it won't make any real difference. We can live as man and wife. We can take assumed names. No one need ever know. And when I die, you'll get the greater share of my money. Will you, darling? *Will you?*"

Kathy, still in his arms, which she noticed now were shaking terribly, stared up into his white, strained face. She saw the sweat breaking out on his forehead. She saw the expression in his eyes. She thought: My lord, he means it. Or he thinks he does.

She patted his cheek playfully. "Charley, you aren't used to taking five highballs at a stretch. I can see that much. Better get yourself together. Take a long, deep breath, honey. Sometimes that helps."

His breath came heavy against her face. "You think I'm drunk. You think I don't know what I'm saying. But I tell you I do know. I do. I haven't had any real fun in life in twenty-five years. I've been tied to a slavish business and a nagging wife. I've almost forgotten what it's like to be happy. I could be happy with you, my darling. Maybe I am drunk. Maybe I'm the kind of fellow who knows better what he wants when he's drunk than when he's sober. Isn't it sensible to want a taste of happiness when you know you may not have much longer to live? Isn't it? Is that such crazy talk?"

Well, no, when he put it like that, perhaps it wasn't really so crazy. Kathy laughed. But the whole idea was out of this world, just the same. She patted his cheek again. "Dream on, honey," she said gently, "if you get any fun out of it. Only it wouldn't work. Even if I were in love with you, it wouldn't work. And I'm not in love with you."

"You might learn to love me," he said wistfully, allowing his hand to touch her bared shoulder. "I'd be awfully good to you," he persisted

"I know you would, honey. But it still wouldn't work. And anyway—" she laughed throatily—"you move too fast for me, Charley. My goodness, I took you for an old slow poke. And now you're way ahead of me. Why, I don't know where I stand from one minute to the next. First you were going to back my dancing act and make me into a howling success. In the next breath we were off on some faraway island."

"It wouldn't have to be an island," Charley said. "California would do. And of course that offer still holds about your career.

I mean, if we can't do the other." He smiled suddenly. "I'd rather do the other, of course. But I've often thought that I'd enjoy being the 'angel' behind a pretty little actress."

Kathy frowned. "You'd find yourself written up in a gossip column before you knew it. You wouldn't like that."

"Why, yes," said Charley, and for a moment he looked quite boyish. "I rather believe I would like it. It would be quite an experience."

Kathy pretended to sigh deeply. "Charley, you're too much for me. You're just a bundle of surprises. Honestly, don't you think you'd better be running along?"

He tried to pull her back into his arms, but Kathy wasn't having any more. "You don't like me," he said unhappily. "I suppose you think I'm just an old fool, and you don't like me.

"I do so like you, Charley. I like you fine." But when he made no move to go on his own power, she got up and found his hat and coat and brought them over to him.

He got up reluctantly and let her help him on with his coat. "You want to get rid of me. You can't get me out fast enough. You don't like me."

She had decided by now that he really wasn't used to drinking so much and it worried her a little. "Would you like me to run down to the corner and call a taxi for you?" she suggested.

No. Charley didn't want a taxi. A dark moroseness seemed to have settled over him. He seemed without interest in taxis, or in life. He started slowly toward the door. "I suppose you won't let me come back again?" he said.

"Why, yes, Charley. You can come back. Why not?"

This seemed to hearten him. And then, as he turned and stood considering her, as his glance feasted once again on those pretty legs in their brief trunks, he seemed still more heartened. She was as lovely as he had thought. And she was asking him to come again. She had said it as if she really meant it, and she was smiling at him. She did have the sweetest smile. Perhaps matters weren't as dark as they looked. Perhaps he had tried to rush her too quickly. After all, he was not accustomed to this sort of thing. It was quite possible that his very eagerness had made her afraid, like a frightened bird scurrying to the wing. He should have moved a little more cautiously.

But she had said there might be a next time, and that gave him hope. That encouraged him. He said, "Do you mind if I kiss you just once more before I go?"

Kathy smiled. She thought that would be okay. But she saw to it that it was the meagerest manner of kisses. She leaned toward him, brushed his cheek with her lips, then pushed him toward the door. "Out with you, wolfie," she said teasingly but firmly.

That amused him. He laughed over it. "Oh," he said, "You're so cute. You're such a darling. And you will let me come again?"

"Didn't I say you could?"

"And you don't dislike me?"

"Of course not, Charley. You're such a dear, how could I dislike you?"

"And that little idea about your dancing career—you will think my proposition over?"

"Of course, Charley." Since he still seemed inclined to linger on and on, Kathy gave him a final push which placed him definitely outside her door. "Didn't I tell you once before? I'm the kind of a girl who will *think* about anything."

CHAPTER FIFTEEN

H E's A FUNNY guy, Kathy thought, when Charley was gone. Smiling to herself, she walked back into the room and lit a cigarette. She stood for a moment smoking it thoughtfully, while her mind ran back over the amusing high points of the last hour. Once she laughed out, and her thoughts were so funny that she decided to run down and see Girlie.

Girlie would enjoy hearing all the racy details about Charley, while they were still fresh in her mind.

She slipped on the green corduroy housecoat, not bothering to lock the door when she went out. As a matter of fact, she had lost the key. But it didn't matter. Locked doors weren't important around the Village.

Girlie looked worried when Kathy came in. It seemed that she had sold all of her "soup tureens." And had she cleaned up on them! She had never had such a good seller. But the problem was where to get hold of some more. She could sell dozens of them, only she didn't have them to sell. And it disturbed her.

Clad in red velvet lounging pajamas, she was lying on the couch and smoking a cigarette through a long holder when Kathy arrived. Girlie said she always did her best thinking when she was in a horizontal position. "Oh, hello there," she said when she saw Kathy. "I'm so glad you came, darling. Where would you go to get more of them if you were me?"

"More of what?" Kathy inquired.

"Oh, you know. Potty-pots. There must be millions of them in this town, stuck away in attics or somewhere. And if I could only get my hands on them, I could make enough to take care of my old age."

Kathy grinned, as she strolled across the room, found one of Girlie's cigarettes and lighted it. "Well, you might start going from door to door, dearie. If it were me, I'd tackle some of those old Fifth Avenue mansions. And when the butler comes to the door you could say, 'Pardon me, but do you happen to have a—' "

"They don't have butlers any more," Girlie interrupted gloomily. "Oh, by the way—" she sat up—"Matt Dexter was in this morning. He left something for you." She went to look for it. "I guess it's that play he's been writing for your erstwhile hunk of sex appeal. Personally, I trust it's lousy. Since as far as I can make out, your wonderful little darling, Tommy, plans to grab all the credit. You're a nice girl, sweetie. I can't find a thing wrong with you, generally speaking, except your taste in lovers. But—I hope you don't mind if I speak frankly—when I think of that Tommy model, I need a clothespin for my nose."

The manuscript was in a large Manila envelope which Matt had sealed. Kathy took it and stared at it. There was no writing on the outside except her name, scribbled in pencil. So Matt had finished with the play and turned it over to Girlie, and he hadn't come near her. "Did he give you any message for me?" she asked in a funny voice.

Oh, yes. Girlie suddenly remembered. "He said something about having to leave hurriedly for California."

"California!"

"That's what he said." She looked at Kathy and her eyes narrowed curiously. "What makes you look so queer, honey? Say, there wasn't anything between you and Matt, was there?"

"Heavens *no*," said Kathy, in extravagant denial. "Me and Matt?" She laughed. "Don't be silly."

"Well, I just wondered. All the time I've been thinking it was you and Tommy and I kept wondering how you could keep on being so dazzled by that piece of nothing on the hoof. But maybe," said Girlie shrewdly, "you've come out of it sooner than I hoped. Oh—I almost forgot—Matt said something about taking a plane." Her eyes were shrewd, smiling a trifle. "If you feel like doing a little plane traveling yourself, I could loan you the money."

"Don't be *silly*," Kathy cried again. Then she left quickly, because she couldn't bear to have Girlie, anyone, guess her sick disappointment.

A plane to California! Well, that was certainly that.

That was the end of Matt Dexter, as far as she was concerned, Kathy said to herself as she went slowly up the stairs to her attic room.

It really was terribly funny, when she thought of all the worrying she had done, about keeping things between herself and Matt on a safe and sensible level. I'll do the guy's play, if I can come in to see you whenever I want, day or night, any old time. And he had never come at all. Not once.

Well, the answer to that one was easy enough. He hadn't wanted to come. He just hadn't wanted to. He had loved her for an hour. He had held her in his arms and looked into her eyes and handed her quite a fancy line. He had made her believe that she meant something special to him—at least for a little while.

And then he had simply lost interest.

It was just a little puzzling as to why he had bothered with Tommy's play, since the idea had been that it was a favor to please her. Oh, well. He had promised to do it. And no doubt he was one of those sticklers for keeping his word, once he had given it. And that, somehow, moved her more than anything. Because it just went to show what a really swell guy he was. He was one in a million, Kathy thought. And for one wonderful night he had taken her into his love. And now he had taken a plane for California. But I don't care, she told herself.

I simply don't give a damn!

And then the tears started, and she hurried on up the stairs to the seclusion of her room so that she could throw herself down and bawl.

"Hi, kid," a gloomy voice said as she opened her door.

Kathy took one look. "Tommy, where did you come from?"

Tommy was seated on the couch, and he was the picture of dejection. He still wore his overcoat and his old slouch hat. The hat looked quite battered indeed. His shoulders were slumped and his eyes looked bleary and, all in all, he might have been a man who had been walking the streets for a night or two.

"Where have you been all this time, Tommy?" Her voice was bright, her smile friendly. The surprise of seeing him had helped her push back the tears.

"Oh. I've been around."

"Aren't you well?"

"Sure, I'm okay, baby."

"Well, you don't look it. As a matter of fact, you look awful. You look like you were just getting over a drunk."

"Well, suppose I am. What the hell about it?"

"Oh, nothing."

"If I want to get drunk, whose business is it? Who the hell cares if I drink myself to death, anyway?"

Kathy stared at him curiously. This was certainly a far cry from the arrogant, independent mood in which Tommy had last left her. "What happened to that job you had?"

Tommy shrugged.

"Well, cheer up, honey." Kathy came across the room to him. "All your worries are over. Here's your manuscript. Matt left it with Girlie this morning. Do you want to open it? Or shall I?"

Tommy shrugged again. "The hell with the damn play," was all he said.

Kathy simply didn't get it. Maybe Tommy was coming down with flu or something. "Well, if you don't want to open it, I will," she said brightly. Her fingers were not quite steady as she broke the sealed strip which fastened it. She kept hoping against hope. Maybe Matt had left some little message for her inside it. He might have done that, mightn't he?

But there was no note for Kathy inside.

In fact, there was nothing inside, except a pile of blank white pages with not a word of any sort on one of them.

Kathy stared, as she ruffled the pages through. They were nice and clean and fresh, just as they had come out of the box. "Well, I'll be darned," she said finally. Then she got angry. If this was Matt Dexter's idea of a joke, it was a mighty crummy one. She wouldn't blame him if he had changed his mind about doing the play. After all, why should he do another man's work for him?

But this—well, this was about the lousiest brand of practical joke she had ever heard of. "I—I could choke him," Kathy said thickly.

Tommy looked around. He hadn't so much as glanced at the package while she was opening it. "There's no play here," Kathy snapped. "There's nothing. I guess this is his idea of being very funny. Oh, Tommy. I'm awfully sorry." And she really was sorry. Here went all of Tommy's fine hopes again.

Tommy smiled for the first time. "You mean he didn't do the thing after all? Oh, well." He didn't seem in the least put out. "Don't worry about it. It doesn't make any difference. That business about the play is all off, anyway."

"What do you mean, it's all off?"

"The Cairn dame changed her mind about financing it. If you must know, she got sore at me. She threw the whole thing up."

Kathy stared at him. 'Why?"

Tommy smiled, rather superciliously. "Oh, it was the same old story. It's always the same with these middle-aged witches. They demand too much of a guy. If you're a little nice to them, they get an idea they own you body and soul. Well, I wasn't having any and I told her so in plain words. I really laid it on the line. And that was that. Why—" he look at Kathy—"do you know what that dame was after? She actually wanted me to trot out to California with her, for an indefinite stay. Can you imagine?"

This version of what had occurred between Tommy and the blonde and fortyish Eunice was a little exaggerated. And yet, to be sure, there was some truth in it. Eunice *had* suggested California. But that was at the beginning of their clandestine stay at the little hideaway in Atlantic City. By the end of a week she had forgotten all about it. And by the end of two weeks she was utterly and completely and forever sick of Tommy. As Eunice invariably sickened of her youthful lovers, once her senses were temporarily satiated. "Get out," she had told him coldly, at the end. "You bore me. Scram."

And that had been the end of Eunice. As it had also been the end of Tommy's bright hopes for the play for which he had, after all, thought up the idea.

Kathy, of course, had no way of knowing all this. She never would know. But the little touch about California really was amusing. The more she thought about it, the more it amused her, and she began to laugh and laugh until she almost lost control.

She really sounded a little hysterical, and when Tommy asked scowlingly what the devil was so funny, it was all she could do to collect herself sufficiently to tell him. "Oh, Tommy," she said, "it's really a scream. Why, it looks like I'm keeping right up with you in your love life."

Tommy glowered. "What have you been doing, you little devil?"

"Oh, I haven't been doing anything. But I've had my chances, brother. Today *I* had an invitation to run off to California. Only mine wasn't to be any temporary arrangement. I was to lie forever and ever and ever in the lap of romantic love with old Charley Whittaker. Can you imagine anything so too ridiculous?"

And then, because she simply had to tell somebody, and she never had got around to confiding in Girlie, she heard herself pouring all the excruciating details into Tommy's angry and suspicious ears. "So now you admit the guy's on the make for you," Tommy snapped. "You aren't making any more bones about it. You admit you had him up here, and he made all these propositions to you. And you—I suppose you just sat like a nice little lady and purred sweetly, 'But, Mr. Whittaker, I'm not that kind of a girl!'

"Like hell you did!" Tommy muttered suddenly. And now, for a moment, he was quite like his old self. Savage in his angry jealousy of her. And out of that jealousy was born a renewal of his old passion for her, and he grabbed her furiously and held her to his lips, and the next few minutes were pretty hectic with Kathy telling Tommy to let her go, and Tommy muttering: "Let you go. Let you go. That's all you have to say to me, when I've been gone for weeks. And all these other guys have stolen my sugar. How many of them have there been? Damn you, how many? Charley Whittaker and how many others?"

As suddenly as it had struck him, Tommy's passion seemed to die out. He let her go and lit a cigarette. An idea seemed to have entered his brain, and for a moment he sat thinking deeply about it. Then he turned back to her and said in the gentlest voice you could imagine: "Sorry, honey. I shouldn't have behaved that way. It's just that I've missed you so. And I get so all-fired jealous of you. I know you're on the level. I know you're true to me. Anyway, true enough."

Now what's struck him? Kathy wondered.

She wasn't long in finding out. Tommy said, his brows drawn as if he were engaged in deep and mighty thought: "You say this Whittaker is interested in—well, in financing my play?"

Kathy shook her head. "I didn't say anything of the sort, Tommy. He's never even heard of you. Mrs. Cairn had been to him, as her banker, to negotiate a loan. I presume she was going to put up security, but she told him about wanting the money to produce a play she was interested in. Then old Charley got the idea that he might take a whirl at financing the play himself, in order to give me a dancing spot in it. Provided I'd play ball with him, of course. He didn't say in so many words that I'd have to become his mistress. But naturally he meant that.

"I doubt if he meant it seriously," she added, after a moment. She grinned. "It was just one of those little situations. I had him sort of bowled over, and he'd had too much to drink, and his ideas sort of ran away with him, if you know what I mean." She giggled. "He certainly was having high, wide, and naughty ideas for a while. I wondered a little if he'd gone clean off his nut."

But Tommy refused to take this lighter and more hilarious view of the situation. Tommy, in fact, saw nothing very funny about it. But he seemed to see a wealth of possibilities in it.

"He wasn't kidding," he said firmly. "I haven't a doubt the old guy was on the level. Why not? Those old boys are always getting a yen for some young lovely. And when they do it, if the girl is smart, it's a simple enough matter to get them to shoot the works. Why don't you get him to do it, honey?"

Kathy stared. "Meaning exactly what, Tommy?" she asked coldly.

"Hell, you know what I mean. Take the old boy up on his offer. Let him finance the play. We'll put a juicy fat dancing part in it for you, and then—why, don't you see, babe? Then we'll both be set. We'll both be on velvet from then on. Don't you see?"

Kathy was afraid that she did see, and now as she looked at Tommy she saw him, for the very first time in all the months she had known him, through eyes from which the veil of her illusions had completely dropped away. She saw him completely and terribly for what he was. Cheap. Weak. A little vile. The kindest thing she could think of him was that he was simply a spoiled, charming weakling who had never grown up. She laughed a trifle. "Well, one objection to all that, Tommy—there isn't any play. Had you forgotten? Matt didn't write it for you."

Tommy brushed that trifle aside. "I'll write the comfounded thing myself," he said. "I can do it, if I set myself to it. Don't let that angle worry you. My Lord, baby, can't you see for yourself?" And he laughed, slapping his leg in his enthusiasm over the outlook. "This is the golden opportunity for both of us. Old Whittaker getting a yen for you right at this time—why, it's the same as striking gold. We'll never get another break like it. We owe it to ourselves to make the most or it."

"Is that the way you look at it, Tommy?"

"It certainly is. Why, *think*. The play may make a lot of dough to start with. And it will make my reputation. All a playwright needs is one hit, and then he can sell anything he writes from there on. I'll never have to worry again. And then, take your angle. You do your stuff, and then Hollywood will be after you. You can write your own ticket. You have the looks, and they'll probably make you a star. We'll both be sitting on top of the world, honey. Right on top of the world! Certainly you wouldn't be such a little fool as to turn your back on all that. You'd be nuts if you did."

"There's one little angle you haven't mentioned," Kathy reminded him coldly. "The catch in it all. Maybe it hasn't even occurred to you that wealthy bankers don't do such wonderful, kind, exciting things for little girls—all for free."

"Oh, well—" Tommy grinned—"suppose you do have to dish up a little fun for the old fellow? It probably won't kill you. He's just an old guy with a lot of young ideas rattling around in his mind. He won't be hard to please. Anyway, baby, you're living in a practical world. And if you want to get on in it, *you've* got to be practical. You've got to make the most of the breaks when they come your way. And there's no two ways about it, Charley Whittaker is certainly one heluva big break. In my language he is."

"Then you wouldn't object to my taking Charley Whittaker for a lover, Tommy?"

Tommy made a wry face and it occurred to him that he needed a drink. He got up to hunt one. "Oh, I'm not saying I *like* the idea, honey. I'm not saying HI *enjoy* it. But I'm too bro-adminded a guy to let my little personal feelings stand in your way. I certainly think enough of you to sacrifice my own selfishness in order to let you forge ahead. I'd be pretty damned selfish if I *tried* to stop you—that's the way I look at it."

"I see, Tommy. You're willing to make the Great Sacrifice. Well, that's certainly big of you, darling. A noble renunciation of self, if ever I heard of one. You should have a medal pinned on you, sweetie." Her voice was heavy with sarcasm, and Tommy didn't like it.

He had found his drink, and he tossed it off hurriedly. "You needn't talk in that tone," he grumbled. "I don't see why you have to leap at every opportunity to put me in the wrong. I'm only trying to think this out on a logical basis. I'm trying to see the big picture."

"And what is the big picture like, Tommy?"

"It's the *future* I'm seeing," Tommy said, "after we've made our killing. You and I, together, from then on. Big shots, both of us. Tommy Terry, the famous playwright. Kathy Neilson, the Hollywood star. The world running after us, instead of the other way around. Set for life. Why, it's wonderful, baby, simply wonderful. Can't you see it the way I do? And what the hell does it matter if we have to put up with a little inconvenience to get started."

"Sure. I see." Kathy smiled tightly. She saw so many things. Charley Whittaker, a little inconvenience. (Such a novel way to put it.) Tommy Terry, the prize heel.

She had put on street clothes and her heavy coat. Now she came over to him, opened her bag, and handed him some money. "I suppose you're broke," she said. "So here's something to buy your dinner with. I won't be home."

He took the money without bothering to thank her. "I hope you won't come to any hasty decision about this, baby," he said. "For heaven's sakes, don't turn the guy down without thinking it all out carefully."

"I won't," Kathy promised sweetly. She walked away from him to the door.

"By the way, where are you going?" Tommy asked. He looked glum. "It's my first night back. I'd have thought you'd have stuck around. Do you have to go?"

"Oh, yes, I have to go," Kathy said. "I have to catch up with my thinking." She gave an odd laugh.

"I've been so taken up with my love life, darling. I've fallen way, way behind in my thinking."

CHAPTER SIXTEEN

SHE HADN'T been thinking straight for months. The victim of her emotions, she'd lost all perspective, let all her fine, beautiful dreams fly out the window, mixed up her life until it was a complete mess. She'd moved into the Village because she thought it would help her to grow artistically. And in a way she had. Her life had developed artistically, after a manner of speaking. As she considered her life now, it looked to her like one of those wacky modern paintings, all leering, grotesque figures, some of them upside down, resembling nothing so much as a nightmare induced by a week-end binge.

And if those pictures were art, then her life was Art. Definitely Art with a capital A.

"I'm just a mess," Kathy decided as she went slowly down the stairs, and by the time she reached the front door she was thoroughly disgusted with herself.

She'd let men pull her this way and that. I'm weak, she decided. Just plain weak. I hate myself. I've a great notion to go somewhere and get tight. Really tight. Stay that way for days and days. Maybe when she came out of it she'd have a little sense.

In this mood, she opened the door leading out and discovered Henry Peterson standing gloomily on the steps. He was huddled in his overcoat and smoking a cigarette. He looked, Kathy thought, rather despondent. It was the first time she had seen Henry in ages. Come to think about it, it was the first she had seen of him since that night when he had barged in on her party like an angry tornado. "Hello, there," she said.

Henry glanced at her then and said: "Oh, hello, Miss Neilson." He gave her a curiously friendly smile, which was surprising. She couldn't remember that he had ever looked really friendly before. "How are you?" he continued. "I haven't seen you for quite a time. Haven't been sick, have you?"

This, for funny Henry Peterson, was being positively garrulous, and Kathy decided that he must have been drinking. Which, in fact, he had. Life had become a bit too much for Henry, and for the very first time in his precise little existence, he had spent a Saturday afternoon in a bar. It had been a pleasurable experience, most pleasurable. And now, back at his own doorstep, he found himself of two minds. He didn't know whether to go on in to Hattie, to endure more of the tongue-lashing which had been his lot of late. Or not to go in.

It was a toughie, all right, trying to decide. So he was standing there in the biting cold, thinking the matter over.

Kathy hesitated. There wasn't much point standing there making conversation with Henry. He had never displayed any especially amiable qualities to her, goodness knows. But by nature Kathy was friendly as a kitten, and always ready to let bygones be bygones. If anyone threw her a friendly smile, she was one to meet them more than half way. So she said: "By the way, Mr. Peterson—I haven't seen you in such a long time—I presume you're in line for congratulations. Did little Junior come along on schedule?"

He gave her a tragic look. "There wasn't any little Junior," he said briefly.

"No Junior?" Kathy's eyes widened. "Well, for heaven's sakes. What happened to him?"

"He wasn't," said Henry grimly. "It was all a mistake. It—well, it turned out that my wife had a tumor."

"Oh, my goodness." And after all of Henry's fussing about, keeping the whole house on pins and needles so as to make sure that Junior would come through safely.

"Well, I am sorry," she said. "And I hope Mrs. Peterson is all right now."

"Oh, yes, she's all right. Physically, I mean. An operation was necessary. But that turned out very successfully. "Henry stared at her for a moment, and it seemed to Kathy that he looked rather wild-eyed. "Only she's been a changed woman ever since. She's hell to live with. Just plain hell, if you know what I mean. I never have any fun."

"Oh, come now," Kathy said brightly. "You mustn't talk like that. You're just feeling sorry for yourself. Everybody has had fun."

"Not me," said Henry grimly.

Abruptly he stopped stock-still right in the middle of the pavement and looked at her earnestly. He shook a finger at her. "Do you know something?" he said.

"What?" asked Kathy.

"I'm just an overgrown boy scout," said Henry darkly. "I've never made love to any woman but my wife. I've never gone out with the boys. I go to work, come home, read the paper, set the alarm, go to bed, get up, go to work, come home—oh, the hell with it," Henry finished.

Kathy was becoming extremely intrigued with this outburst. Henry was beginning to fascinate her. "Do you know what I think?" She smiled. "I think you've been out with the boys today."

"No, I haven't."

"Well, then you've been doing a little solitary drinking. And that's bad. You should always take someone along when you go drinking."

To which Henry replied astonishingly: "Well, how about you coming along and doing a little drinking with me?"

Kathy arched her brows, pretending extreme disapproval. "Why, Mr. Peterson," she drawled. "What would your wife say?"

"I don't give a good bloody damn what she says," snorted Henry.

Kathy giggled, over a sudden idea. Impulsively, she tucked her own hand under Henry's arm. "Know what you ought to do?" she said. "Go out and get drunk and stay away for a couple of nights. Let that babe stew in her own juice. If you scared her badly, got her afraid you'd gone for good and weren't coming back, it might teach her a lesson."

Henry was immediately receptive to this idea. "Maybe you've got something there," he said thoughtfully. "By gosh, maybe you have. I've never stayed away from Hattie for a single night, not in all the years we've been married." He laughed.

"That's bad," Kathy said. "Every man ought to stay away for a night every now and then. My goodness, Henry." And she giggled. "Didn't anyone ever tell you? A woman doesn't like to be too sure of a man."

"You're right," said Henry firmly. "And that's where I've made my mistake. I've let Hattie be too sure of me. I've let that woman walk right smack over me. And now she's so sure of me, she just treats me like—well, like a bloody worm."

"Well, which are you? A man or a worm?"

"I'm a man, by heaven," said Henry. "And by gosh, I'll show her I'm a man." He became irresolute, as a new thought struck him. He looked around at Kathy. "Only if I'm going to stay out all night, I ought to have a girl to stay with me. Oughtn't I?"

Kathy thought. "Of course, that's the accepted procedure. But I don't suppose it's absolutely necessary. I mean—you could stay away, and your wife could imagine you were with a woman, but you wouldn't really have to have one."

Henry shook his head. No. He didn't quite like that idea. If he was going to cut loose for once in his life, he wanted really to cut loose. He wanted to do the thing up brown and no pretending about it. His argument was that he wouldn't feel right, letting Hattie think he was with a girl, if he wasn't really with one. And anyway, he'd never stayed out with a girl. All his life he'd heard other men talk about their little affairs on the side and he had never done anything like that. Now he felt that he'd like to do it.

Once more, he made one of his abrupt stops in mid-pavement. "How about you going somewhere with me for the night?" he suggested. And he wasn't as shy or embarrassed about it as you might have expected.

Kathy stared. "Me? *Me*, Henry? Oh, my goodness." She wanted terribly to laugh. "I'm sorry," she said weakly, "but I couldn't. I just couldn't."

"Why not?" Henry caught her arms roughly, and his eyes, in the late twilight, looked shiny as dark blue beads. "Why couldn't you? You're one of these Village girls. You're used to doing unconventional things. You have boys with you at all hours of the night. Why couldn't you go somewhere with me for the night?"

"I'm sorry, but I just couldn't."

"You don't like me enough," Henry said sadly. "That's the reason, isn't it? Maybe I'd never find a girl who would like me enough."

"Oh, I'm sure you would. They're not so hard to find."

"You don't like me," Henry persisted. "Maybe you're sore at me because I used to complain about the noise you made. It was my wife keeping after me that made me complain. She made me call the police that night. Now you blame me—

"But the police never showed up after all," Kathy laughed. "Besides, I never hold a grudge. I'm not blaming you for a thing and I'm not sore. Only—"

"Only you just don't like me. I'm miserably unhappy and I need cheering up, but you don't like me well enough to go some place with me and cheer me up."

Kathy gave his arm a friendly pat, then caught him and drew him along down the street.

Jerry's basement bar was at the next corner. She could see the flickering lights over the doorway as they came toward it. "I'll tell you what," she said. "We'll go into Jerry's and have a couple of drinks. That will cheer you up. Maybe it will cheer me up, too," she added, suddenly remembering that she had troubles of her own.

"I can sympathize with you more than you know," she told Henry consolingly. "I know all about how it feels, when your life gets in a complete mess."

"You do?"

"I certainly do."

"But you're young. You have your whole life before you. And anyway, you couldn't possibly have made the kind of mistakes I've made.... "

"Not the same kind," Kathy admitted gloomily. "But worse ones than you ever dreamed about." This was after they were seated in Jerry's and well advanced on their second whiskey and soda.

"That," said Henry, "I don't believe. No one ever made worse mistakes than I've made. No one. Do you know where I made my big mistake? I should have told that witch where to get off years ago. I should have told her right out who was wearing the pants in our house. But no, I let her get the upper hand."

"Where I made my mistake," said Kathy dismally, "was in being born. If I had never been born, I would never have made any other mistakes. Because," she added brightly, "I wouldn't have been here to make them, would I?"

And over their fourth or fifth whiskey: "If I had never been born, I would never have got in With this bunch of Village bums to start with. I would never have let that lousy, good-for-nothing sponger, Tommy Terry, use me for a meal ticket. And I would never have fallen in love with a man who scrammed out on a plane for California without so much as telling me goodbye.... "

Where the time had gone to, Kathy never could remember afterwards. Nor how in the world it got to be way after mid-night. But it was. And there she and Henry were, still in Jerry's bar. And Kathy was confessing to Henry, and to herself for the very first time, that Matt Dexter was the man she loved.

"He's the only man I'll ever love," she told Henry earnestly. "Positively the only one. Oh, he's such a wonderful man. And he was a hero. Did I tell you he was a hero?"

Yes, Henry said, she had told him that several times.

"And he's a genius too," Kathy explained. "He writes the most wonderful stories about the war. They're so real, so *alive.*" She was not deterred in her enthusiasm by the fact that she had never seen one of Matt's stories. "He really writes. He doesn't just talk about it. And he really gets published. He doesn't just dream about it. And, oh, Henry, I love him so. I'll love him to my dying day. I nearly swoon every time I think about him. But he doesn't care that about me." And she snapped her fingers. "He doesn't know I'm alive. Did I tell you?" she demanded drearily, for about the tenth time. "He just took a plane for California, and never even said goodbye. He never even said goodbye."

At this point in her alcoholic confessional, Kathy's underlip began to quiver and tears filled her lovely eyes.

"Poor little girl," Henry said. "You poor, dear, lovely little darling. That guy ought to be shot, walking out on you like that. I can't imagine any man treating a nice little girl like you so—so outrageously."

"Don't you start criticizing Matt," Kathy rose instantly to his defense. "He didn't do anything outrageous. He just didn't have any time for me. He couldn't see me for dust. He thought I was just another little tramp and—and I guess he was right. Oh, Henry, how am I to bear it? Never to see him again. Never, never, never.... "

Henry slid his chair around so that he could put his arm comfortingly around Kathy. No one in the bar paid any attention. Jerry's midnight customers were invariably broadminded and without great curiosity. If a girl wanted to cry into her drinks and the man wanted to comfort her, it was okay by them. It was nothing to stare at.

"He'll be back," said Henry, who had quite forgotten his own problems. It was such a novel experience for him, having a lovely young thing pour her sorrows into his ear. Nothing of the sort had ever happened to him before and he was quite enjoying it. "Don't you worry, honey. He'll come back."

"Do you really think so?" Kathy lifted her drowning, wondrous eyes to Henry's. "Do you really think I'll ever see him again?"

"Why, of course you will. How could a man stay away from you? A man you cared about? Why—" Henry seemed suddenly overcome with a staggering thought—"If a lovely girl like you were in love with me, the way you are with this other guy, I'd cross burning deserts and snow-capped mountains to get to you. I'd *fly* to you on the wings of love."

That was a pretty thought and Kathy considered it for a moment. Then impulsively she flung her arms around Henry.

"Oh," she said, "you're the sweetest thing. You're just a quaint, cute, sweet little old dear—"

And it was just then that the door of Jerry's Cocktail Palace opened and something in the nature of a tidal wave rushed in.

It was a tall, bony woman with a long horse face and a bad eye if ever Kathy saw one. And the woman came toward them in such a rush that Kathy, whose vision was momentarily a trifle blurred, didn't at first recognize the man who followed her.

The woman planted herself beside their table, and Kathy said playfully: "Hi, Horsie-face. Somebody put the bite on you?"

"What," said the woman, "are you doing with my husband?"

"You mean Henry? Is Henry your husband?" Kathy giggled. "Now I've seen everything. No wonder the man hates to come home to you. Look, Horsie, did you ever try a beauty parlor? They couldn't work any miracles on a face like yours, but they might help."

And then Kathy saw the man strolling toward her. Saw him more clearly. Saw Matt.... "Oh," she said weakly.

Matt grinned crookedly. "Hi, Kathy," he said. "Ready to go home?"

Kathy started to get up. *Matt had come back.* She couldn't believe it. Maybe she was dreaming. But her eyes, clinging to him, held a wonderful brightness. And she had completely forgotten poor Henry, who was now looking very uncomfortable indeed.

She remembered him suddenly, however, when his loving spouse began hurling acid invectives at him. "Why, you little so-and-so," the light of Henry's life was rasping, "I ought to kill you. I ought to divorce you. What do you mean—leaving me at home to worry about you, while you run about slopping up liquor with this little trollop?"

This unkind remark brought Matt into action. Kathy had got up, moving slowly toward Matt like a woman in a trance.

And now Matt put not too gentle hands on Mrs. Henry Peterson and pushed her roughly down into the chair which Kathy had vacated. "Shut up, you," Matt said. "One more crack like that out of you and I'll shake you until your teeth rattle. Understand?"

Which remark, in turn, brought Henry belatedly in mind of his duties as a husband. He popped to his feet, his plump cheeks shaking. "See here, sir." He jerked worriedly at Matt's arm. "Don't you dare talk that way to my wife. You take your hands off her. Do you hear me? Take your hands off."

"Okay. But tell your wife to watch her lip," Matt said pleasantly. "If she were a man, I'd slap her down for what she just said. Since she isn't—" Matt stood for a second, regarding Henry, and the longer he looked the less he seemed to care for what he saw— "and since she was right up to a point—after all, why were you in here getting tight with my girl?—I'll just sock you instead."

And Matt gave Henry a left to the jaw which sent the little man spinning dazedly and helplessly to the floor. "I simply yielded to an irresistible impulse," Matt told Kathy when they were outside. "Anyway, the little guy had it coming." He looked at Kathy sternly. *"After all,* what was he doing out with my girl?"

Kathy still had the sensation that she was spinning way up in the clouds. But no longer because of the liquor. No delirium induced by a few too many drinks was ever so breathlessly wonderful as this. It was a starless night, but Kathy was walking among the stars. They walked along the narrow, shabby street, which was quite devoid of beauty, and yet Kathy had never known such beauty. *Matt had come back.* She said faintly: "Since when am I your girl, Matt?"

"Since the beginning of time," said Matt extravagantly, putting his arm around her, holding her to him as they walked. "Certainly since that first day, when I came up to your apartment and you—"

"But you went away," Kathy reminded him. "You didn't come near me. And then you went away without a word. And I thought I would never see you again."

"Did that worry you?" Matt asked eagerly. "Did you care at all—knowing I might never come back?"

"It worried me something awful." Kathy laughed softly. "Now that you're here, I almost forget how terrible it was. But you can see for yourself. It was so bad, it sent me out on a binge with Henry Peterson. Doesn't that show you?"

Matt laughed. "It shows something or other, and that's a fact." Then, quickly serious: "I haven't been near you because I wanted to see if I could stay away. I didn't want to fall for any girl. I didn't want to fall for you. But my work went to pot on account of you. Then I tried to lose myself in that derned play. That wouldn't go either. I didn't leave you those blank pages just to be funny. I thought maybe you'd get the point. No matter what I tried to do, I drew a blank. Because all I could see, all I could think of, was you. I got so damned sore at myself. You seemed to have me bewitched. And I'd be darned if I was going to be bewitched by any Village lovely. That's what I said to myself. So I decided to run away. Only that didn't work out. The plane had to make a forced landing outside of Chicago."

He grinned down at her. "I decided that was an omen of some sort. Or maybe I just decided to give in. I had a yen for you, I was stuck with it, and suddenly there just didn't seem any sense in fighting it any longer."

"Well, that was sensible of you," Kathy said sweetly, her eyes in his, her body hugged close to him as they walked slowly along. She giggled suddenly. "*The Man Who Came Back*. That sounds like Tommy's play, doesn't it? Maybe you should write a play about us. But look—how did you ever happen to team up with

Henry Peterson's wife? How did you happen to come looking for me at Jerry's?"

Matt shrugged. "When I got back to the house, things were in an uproar. The Peterson dame was rushing about, telling everybody that her husband hadn't come home and she suspected he'd gone away with a woman. Girlie was trying to get her calmed down. Then we went up to your room, and there was *your* boy friend having himself a crying drunk and blahing that you'd walked out on him. There was a lot of nutty talk, and finally I tried to quiet la Peterson down by telling her I'd go out and hunt around the Village hot spots for her little darling. I started, and she insisted on tagging along. And here I am."

They came to a corner, and Matt stopped. He put both his arms around her. "I haven't kissed you for a long, long time, sweetheart," he said softly.

"Not for several eternities," Kathy whispered shakily.

So he kissed her and she was bathed in rapture and wonder until the sweetness and ecstasy seemed more than she could endure. She lifted her head, her voice tremulous. "Matt, are you going to fight it any more?"

"Fight loving you?" He seemed a little savage in his intensity. "What the hell's the use? I can't fight it. Now the question is—am I going to have to slug it out with a certain other guy to get you all for myself? Honey, do you still love him?"

"Meaning Tommy?" Kathy threw back her head and laughed. It was almost impossible to believe she had ever imagined she loved Tommy. "No," she said. "Heavens, no. That was never love," she added. "Just a mild form of insanity."

"I'm glad you've found it out," Matt said tightly. "But I'm not taking any chances. You're leaving now, see? With me. You're not even going back to pack your stuff. Let him wonder what happened to you. Some day you can write him that you're married.

"Married? Oh, Matt."

"Sure. *Marriage.* Never hear of it? I know it isn't an old Village custom. But you may enjoy it, once you get used to it. Tonight I'll get you a hotel room, and first thing Monday—"

Kathy's arms tightened around him. "Marriage on Monday sounds swell, darling. But that hotel room tonight—will it be a room for two?"

"Well, of course, if you insist—"

"I do insist, sweetheart. I'm still a Village gal at heart." She laughed. "And I do so yearn for one wonderful night before I go all out for the conventions."

"What I'm going to teach you about wonderful nights—" Matt grinned at her—"baby, you've no idea."

THE END